To Mama With Love

A Family Affair

Anthony Sharp

To Susan

my very special niece

Chapter 1

She was sipping her aperitif and thinking about lunch when she spotted him: a tall, good-looking man, still in his thirties - sporting a well-cut suit, striped shirt and youthful coiffure. Casually he glanced around the bar, and turned from his drinking partner to take another look at her. Two could play this game. She was desirable, he had to admit: striking features, great body and hair, and warm, intelligent eyes – now focused on his. He smiled. She returned the compliment, and waited for the fun to begin. It was not long before he took leave of his pal and walked across to introduce himself.

His voice, rich and mellifluous, waved a magic wand over her, making it difficult to place its origin. 'Hello. May I invite you and your friend to a drink and perhaps… a smidgen of lunch?'

A piano tinkled in the background, and the pianist had begun to croon her favourite song.

'Amanda is the name...' She surprised herself as she held out her hand for him to clasp and gently caress. Their eyes glistened, and Amanda's friend knew she would soon have to make a decent exit to allow love its head. She'd stay merely to witness the rest of the opening scene.

'Carl Himmler, at your service.'

Amanda could scarcely believe her ears, and as a discernible shiver passed along her spine, she swore she could hear a clicking of the heels together with the now unmistakable German accent. But his face was so gorgeous, his eyes full of life and joy, his body simply... Well, he was nothing like the pictures she'd seen years ago of Heinrich Himmler, the notorious mass murderer of the SS. This beautiful man in front of her couldn't be of the same family, surely?

Her eyes spoke of their own accord: yes, they said. She would go the whole way with him, even though his very name shot her an uncomfortable twinge of guilt. Yes, she'd go all the way with this Carl Himmler, even if she disobeyed her own father, now ensconced in his successful showbiz agency in The States. Would he ever forgive her? If she were to be foolish or defiant enough to marry the man, would he kill her? For David Davidson was pure Jewish and proud of it. He had worked hard to build his business, and had long ago moved offices to New York where he felt at home - smoking his big, fat cigars, and dining in Sardi's at least twice a week.

They had sat down to lunch, just the two of them. Amanda's friend had quietly disappeared, and Carl's drinking pal was nowhere to be seen. They were on their own and free to pursue the game. For life, if they so wished. But words would prove inadequate to describe the drama that was destined to unfold, long after Amanda had let loose her sexual desires with Carl, and married him within the year. How could David Davidson foresee that, after bringing two wholesome children into the world his daughter would give birth to a third but loathsome child who'd bring distress and shame upon the whole family? Yet David was an intelligent man who had experienced life in most of its colours. For better or for worse he'd had his share of trouble before moving to America. His wife had died of cancer at the age of forty-nine; his son, Amanda's elder brother whom they'd all adored left the mortal coil from epilepsy when he was a mere twenty-five, and Amanda herself had chosen to stay behind in London to pursue, in her words, "the life of refined culture". Not for her the bright lights of New York or even a gaudy house in Bishops' Avenue, Hampstead, lit up for all the world to gawp at. Her taste was English, subtle: a small, elegant Georgian terraced house, rubbing shoulders with the others in Brompton Square.

This her father could accept, if it made her happy. His fortune would go to her, anyway. But would he change his mind if Amanda persisted with her new German beau? Would he change his mind about remarrying? He had seemed so adamant that he would not. As far as he was concerned, he had said, it was a device for desperate men. He was not desperate, despite his painful losses. His business-brain would rule him, not his fluttering, broken heart. Positive he would remain, and join in the fun of a crazy world when he chose. But would everything change if she insisted pursuing the German?

They were on their main course of rack of lamb and sauté potatoes when Amanda's curiosity got the better of her.

'But what do you really do, Carl?'

They had raised their glasses of fine Burgundy, and clinked them with a smile.

'I don't think you'd want to know, Amanda. It's not a particularly pretty pursuit. Not as colourful, I'd say, and not as much fun as I imagine your boutique to be.'

'Tell me, all the same.'

'I manufacture armaments. And I make money.'

She lowered her glass from her lips, and did her best to respond without shock or censure.

'Well, everyone is entitled to a living. It would not be my choice, but I try not to be too judgemental in life.'

'Good. You are not only intelligent, but pragmatic. And very beautiful, if I may say so. A rare combination, Amanda.'

Other women would have felt flattered. But Amanda could read people's motives, and separate truth from falsehood. Till now. His words, like hers, were cool, but her heart continued to pound. Who was this super-looking guy, wining and dining her? Who did he really work for? Was the mafia involved?

Her father had had an odd brush with the mob in his New York office, some years back. But he was so quick on the draw and on the appropriate buttons that it ended up with them all having a drink and a laugh together.

This was different: armaments for the world to play with, and a German 'in control' with the name Himmler. The mind boggled. But her desire for him persisted.

If she told her father, would he kill her with his bare hands, die of shock, or simply end it all after a large, rich meal and a bloody good piss-up in his club? And if she managed to hide the truth from him, could she live with her conscience? Who could she turn to if the situation got out of hand?

He had homed into her thoughtful face, and picked up the scent of concern.

'Don't look so worried, Amanda. Everything is going to be fine. I'm a very good businessman, though I say so myself. I can take care of most things, and I'd certainly look after you - if you'd allow me the privilege.'

She smiled on him, and the tension broke up. Her worries she would shelve for another day. What the hell. She needed to let go occasionally. She was a hardworking woman who deserved some fun. Her boutique, a stone's throw from Harrods, featured her own designs which were fast becoming the talk of the town, and she had left her staff clear instructions to carry on without her for the afternoon. So why shouldn't she give herself a break? Besides, she was already quite rich in modern terms. Not only did she own the terraced house in Brompton Square, but she had bought some land and nice property in France, and put the rest of the money into a Swiss bank account. She had plans to remove that to an even safer haven should the European authorities be foolish enough to tax it. She wasn't Jewish for nothing.

'Come on, Amanda,' continued Carl, 'Let's have some fun.'

Another bottle of Burgundy appeared on the table. And for Amanda, life had only just begun.

Chapter 2

The weeks flew by, and she could not remember ever having had so much fun. The sex was simply wonderful, the wining and dining world-class, and the travel and entertainment sufficient to keep the average woman's head spinning for years.

But Amanda was anything but average. She had let her hair down, not least in order to stoke up the energy for the next bout of hard work which she sensed loomed on the horizon. Whether or not she tussled with her father over the affair with Carl or went even further and married the man and produced a family, she would need all the energy she could muster.

Five weeks after she'd met Carl, she plucked up the courage to tell her father of her involvement. As expected, David Davidson exploded:

'What? You silly bitch. What are you trying to do to me, Amanda?'

'Calm down, dad. Times have changed since your day. I love the man. He's intelligent, kind, attentive, and...'

'Attentive? I'll tell you what he's attending to. Presumably he knows you have that house in

Knightsbridge, the boutique, the designs, property in Fr...'

'I've not told him about France, or my Swiss bank account, or...'

'And you think he's not clever enough to find out exactly what he needs to know? What's he do for a living?'

'Manufactures armaments. Worldwide.'

'Holy Moses. You'll be telling me next he sells 'em to the God-dam Arabs.'

'Of course, dad. Anyone with the money.' Amanda had always enjoyed being provocative towards her father when she felt the urge. Besides, he seemed to welcome the challenge.

'You're not serious, Amanda?'

'Couldn't be more serious.'

'My God. I gotta take a pill. This is gettin' out of hand.'

David Davidson swallowed his prescribed pill with a swig of water and continued: 'Look, Amanda. A joke's a joke. You carry on with this Kraut at your own peril. I wash my hands of the whole thing, and you force me, you understand, to rethink my position towards your good self.'

'You mean you're cutting me off without a cent?'

'You have the house, the boutique, cash in the bank, property in old Europe. What more do you need?'

'Your approval, father, and your love.'

'My love you have for ever, Amanda. My support if you're in trouble. Everything a good Jewish father should guarantee his daughter. But my money is my money. I'm not averse to a spot of moral blackmail if it comes to it, my dear. So, think hard.'

'I am thinking, father. And to prove you will never have to put your blackmailing into practice, I intend to marry Carl.'

A stony silence prevailed over the line, and Amanda wondered whether her father had collapsed in an apoplectic fit or had merely put down the phone piece during all the noise he was making. But he came back on board and tried a softer approach.

'Look, Amanda. You go ahead with your life. I know you have sharp instincts and will no doubt pull out of the affair at the slightest sign of trouble. I think you know what I mean.'

'I know what you mean, father. And don't worry. I have, as you say, sharp instincts. I shall take all necessary precautions while subtly delving into character, CV and past. But history is history, dad. The Germans have moved on.'

'Yeah, pull the other one. And it's a damned shame no one takes the trouble to teach you kids a bit of history, these days.'

Amanda smiled to herself at her father's words and ingrained sentiments. She was intent upon proving a good man remained a good man, no matter his origin and background.

But her father had not finished... 'And those armaments worry me, Amanda. What sort of a guy gets mixed up in that trade?'

'Someone who will supply Israel, too, dad?'

''Um. You know how to touch the weak spots, don't you, my girl?'

Amanda allowed herself another smile, and wrapping up the conversation, turned on her special balming voice: 'Father, I love you. Please don't worry. I'll keep you posted on events. And look after yourself.'

'You ain't making it easy.'

'Oh, come on, dad. Save the blackmail for a few of your awkward clients over there.'

David laughed down the line. He was proud of his daughter, and despite his understandable prejudices he felt sure Amanda would come up trumps. If she couldn't convert a typical German to her way of thinking, then no one could. He'd give her the benefit of the doubt. If she went ahead with the wedding, he might even agree to turn up. If asked. Not that he'd encourage such an event.

'Do be careful, Amanda. God bless you. Shalom.'

'Bless you, too, father. Shalom.'

Before the year was out... The wedding took place in Westminster Cathedral. Carl had always been a

14

Catholic. He'd never considered himself particularly religious, but his parents had remained devout and anxious their son should find his feet in a thoroughly tested organization. For them 'The Da Vinci Code' was a long way off. And Hitler merely a fallen angel.

Amanda even converted to Catholicism to keep things sweet and prove to Carl and his parents that Jesus wasn't the only Jew to step out of line. What a turn-up for the books, she had said. Well, Amanda could do the same.

Much to her delight, her father David Davidson stepped out of a new Rolls-Royce, beaming broadly and throwing open his massive arms to hug her tight. Some of the Germans appeared a trifle embarrassed by such a display of overt Jewish affection, but Carl smiled warmly and proceeded to give David a hug of his own. They held each other, and looked into one another's eyes. Instantly, Amanda's father could read the soul and character of the young man before him...Carl Himmler was no Nazi, even if he'd found himself in a spot of trouble with the police as a typical, rebellious, spunky youngster. Carl's eyes were kind. Yes, clear, bright and blue. But kind and sincere. His parents also seemed open and generous in spirit. Nothing like David expected or feared.

The service began with an uplifting hymn set to the music of Haydn. Holy Moses, wasn't this the German National anthem? David Davidson began to sweat and then remembered it was a tune he'd heard on an odd occasion years before in a very English church in Somerset. Not a German could be seen for miles that day.

Calm down, David, he told himself...

Then the ceremony began: 'Dearly beloved, we are gathered here to witness the union of this couple Carl Himmler and Amanda Davidson in Holy Matrimony.'

When it came to the point where an objection to the union could be raised, David froze...

'Or forever hold his peace,' said the priest. This was David Davidson's chance to obstruct the ceremony and ruin Amanda's day. A perverse desire came over him to do just that: it's show business, he'd tell 'em afterwards. But the moment had passed, his chance to put a stop to a very unlikely union. His daughter, his only daughter had gone and married a Kr... He pulled up and gave himself a symbolic slap on the wrist. His mind was in a daze as he glanced across to the Best Man - a friend of Carl called Fritz who stood erect in his dark suit and clicked his heels (David could have sworn) as he passed the ring to Carl to slip on Amanda's finger. The promises were made - delivered in immaculate English, and the priest continued:

16

'I pronounce Carl and Amanda man and wife...
Let no man put asunder.'

Chapter 3

Holy God, could this be happening before his eyes - his only daughter, Jewish as they come, marrying a German with the name of Himmler? What had he done, giving his consent, travelling across the Atlantic to give her away? His darling daughter Amanda...

The couple smiled and kissed affectionately, and the bride turned towards her father with a radiant face. She looked beautiful. And happy. So happy. What could David her father do except wish her all the best, and let go? The organ burst forth in a stunning performance of Bach's Toccata and Fugue in D minor. The congregation remained in their seats and listened. This, at least, was an educated lot, thought David. Maybe his fears were completely unfounded, and he should open his eyes to the new Germany and the new generation. He'd always been a fair man, if decidedly old-fashioned. He made up his mind to give it a go. If Amanda could be brave enough to do what she'd done, the least he could do would be to give her his support.

'Come on, David. You look so pensive. Have a drink.' Carl passed his father-in-law a glass of fine champagne. And they clinked glasses. The reception was about to become one of the best The Savoy had witnessed.

The food was out of this world, the wine divine, and the cake - a magnificent three-tiered monster with delicious, succulent flavours.

'Too good for Hitler,' pronounced Carl's father, sitting next to David.

'You couldn't have known him, surely?'

'No. But my own father was in The Hitler Youth and met the bastard quite often. Always suspected Hitler had a soft spot for my dad. He was a good-looking boy, judging by the photos.'

David smiled at the old man's openness and acceptance of human proclivities.

'"There's nowt so queer as folk", they say in England.'

'Oh, yes, your English humour and subtlety of language. I do admire it. So, what are you doing in America?'

David laughed out loud. He had begun to loosen up and enjoy himself. And as their conversation developed, ranging from philosophy, music, art, science, world politics to business, they both seemed to have forgotten where they were. Carl and Amanda's wedding reception might just as well have been on the moon. A loud tap on a glass jolted the two men to the reality of the occasion.

SPEECH, SPEECH…David Davidson was called upon to give his daughter away again - in the speech of his life. Could he do it? Would he do it? Among all these Germans? Ah, what the hell? His daughter was happy. The war long gone. He'd entered into conversation with one of the most delightful men he'd met in years. Carl seemed kind, bright and alert. His parents most civilized. Germany was now locked into Europe, had given money to Israel to assuage her guilt. She was working hard for peace and reconciliation. Who was David Davidson, a lucky, rich bastard living in The States to grumble about the past?

Before he'd reached the podium to deliver his speech, he was feeling pretty good about life. His daughter appeared deliriously happy. Carl, too. Everyone present looked in fine shape, and eager to hear his words.

Smiles and clapping greeted his 'entrance'. Here goes, he said to himself... 'Ladies and Gentlemen, boys and girls, friends and acquaintances… It is the custom in England for the father of the bride to address the gathering at the reception, and usually bore the pants or knickers off you.' Laughter and grins greeted this remark, and David continued, much encouraged… 'I confess to you good people that even while crossing the Atlantic to attend Amanda's wedding, I harboured doubts as to the wisdom of her love and commitment to Carl. But when I came face to face with this charming young man (here David

20

smiled benignly upon his son-in-law), my fears subsided. For I can see he is a man of integrity, and I feel sure he will make Amanda happy for years to come.'

As applause broke out among the guests, Amanda's tears of joy were complemented by a loving kiss from Carl, and David went on: 'And I wish to thank him and his family for receiving and embracing The Davidson's - an unashamedly Jewish lot!' (kind laughter followed this remark) 'And to prove I am no longer prejudiced, I have bought Carl and Amanda a brand new Steinway Grand Piano. Is that all right?'

David turned to face Carl and Amanda who whistled their approval and gratitude, but he had more to say: 'I could, I suppose, have insisted upon a New Yorker, but in deference to the German connection, I have chosen a Hamburger!'

A naughty grin etched David's face, and not a few of the guests expressed their appreciation of the pun.

'I know Carl has a number of talented friends who play piano. Besides, perhaps Amanda will now take her music a little more seriously.'

'Oh, dad. You are wicked.' Amanda smiled on her father, so pleased and relieved was she that he seemed to fit in so well with the scene, mingling effortlessly with Carl's family and circle of German friends. Yet she knew how clever he really was. Could this current good humour and velvet touch be a smoke-screen for his own serious enquiries into Carl's nature and business? She could already sense he would not entirely be happy until Carl found himself involved in a more artistic and morally acceptable trade than armaments. The internet had made the whole business of armaments appear such a matter of fact, normal shopping list. But anyone with a brain knew about the arms dealers, the black market, the shady characters who lurked behind the scenes and plied their ruthless trade as if they were skinning a cat. David himself could never forget the sudden death of a close friend, soon after that friend had brokered a huge deal between two leading banks - cross continents. That was just money - okay, black money, perhaps, but money nevertheless. If a bank could rub out a middle man just like that, how much more expected would be the death of an arms dealer.

'But I'm not an arms dealer,' protested Carl after the speeches and wedding feast. He had invited David to his rooms in The Savoy for a chat - while Amanda was getting herself spruced up for the honeymoon. 'I am a manufacturer. A huge difference, David. If some of my arms get into the wrong hands, it is, I fear, only to be expected - in this day and age. But think about defence. Surely the defence of honourable nations is important, too?'

'Yes indeed, Carl. But what about your personal safety? Can you not be bribed?'

'I am covered, not only by my own strict rules but by the company rules of conduct. The export controls are pretty tight, and our licence would be revoked if we were caught stepping out of line. I am determined, David, that we should keep our side of the bargain.'

'Good man, Carl. You have said your piece, and I am satisfied. No more questions.'

'Until after the honeymoon, you mean?' Carl grinned at David who winked and pulled contentedly on his cigar.

'You have a wonderful time, my boy. And forget about this old fart, here. Amanda knows I worry about everything. You must forgive my intrusions.'

'There is nothing to forgive, David. I would never insult your intelligence. It would be unreasonable to expect you not to question the wisdom of my union with Amanda. It's not every day one meets an arms manufacturer, let alone an arms dealer.'

David Davidson pulled again on his cigar, and took it from his mouth thoughtfully...'I'm not sure an arms manufacturer and a Steinway Grand go together, despite Steinway's 'experiences' in World War 2.' The two men laughed out loud. 'Take good care of her, son.'

'Who? The Steinway or Amanda? Carl's quick repartee made David laugh anew.

'They've both cost me money, I can tell you. You or I could replace the Steinway. But Amanda is irreplaceable. Wouldn't you agree?'

'No question of it. I shall do all in my power to make her happy. Your lovely daughter is a one-off, and I am honoured to have her as my wife. I thank you for ever.'

'What are you two rattling on about? Come on, Carl. We'll be late.' Amanda had emerged from the bathroom, ready and eager to get going.

'It's our honeymoon, darling. Not a bloody trade fair.' Carl winked at David who grinned with broad understanding. He was warming to his son-in-law more by the second.

Chapter 4

Within the year, The Himmlers had produced their first child.

Carl remained easy-going about the name of his son, but as Amanda cradled baby Adam in her arms and gently rocked him to sleep, she remembered why she'd always liked the name.

She began to hum her favourite carol, 'Adam lay ybounden' by Boris Ord. Instinctively she knew this to be a rare moment of reflection: the future would give her little opportunity for anything other than practical considerations. Her soul, thank God, would remain intact, but her contemplative side would have to take a back seat for some while to come...

Right now, almost as though directed by a higher authority, her mind drifted back to a very special occasion years before, when, as a girl, she had been invited to attend The Festival of Nine Lessons and Carols in the chapel of King's College, Cambridge. Her Christian school-friend had an uncle who was a don at the college. Two tickets were then acquired for the girls who found themselves "transported to Heaven" before they had even settled into their seats near the choir-stalls. As the magnificent organ sounds subsided and faded into the ether to make way for the eerie but beautiful voice of the lone chorister singing Once in Royal David's City, Amanda thought of her beloved father David, Jewish to the core. Her mind turned to Jesus, Jewish by birth, but destined to unleash the extraordinary new faith that would transform the world - for better or for worse: too often, alas, it would be for the latter. While wicked, ignorant men would make war and profit by the confusion and division of faiths, Church and State would collude and trample on the freedoms and hopes of good, thinking people who dared question the authorities.

Now here she was, changed into a Catholic. Just like that. Could it have been that easy? Perhaps it was for the best, thought Amanda. If there is but one God, why does he have to have so many different faces? She stopped herself going mad. There was work to do. The baby's nappies needed changing. Fast.

The years seemed to fly by, for the marriage was a great success, and their love for each other, if anything, increased with the passage of time. Young Adam grew to be a credit to both his parents and to Brompton Oratory Choir School - where he shone as a bright pupil with personality and a beautiful treble voice. Handsome, physically strong, yet sensitive and artistic, he had everything going for him. As he matured, his father took him on trips abroad to see something of the world, while Amanda looked after her boutique and their second child, Sally, born a year and a half after her brother. She, too, had stunning looks. Instinctive and vivacious, she nevertheless possessed a thoughtful, kind side to her - ever sensitive to any hurt her actions would provoke in other people. An extraordinary girl, not unlike her mother when she was a child.

Then, one day, when Adam was around twelve and a half and Sally eleven years old, a dramatic change shook the Himmler household. Life, somehow, would never be quite the same again...

Amanda had had a particularly busy week, and she felt she deserved a tiny break on her own. She had returned to the house in Brompton Square, and was about to sit down to read a few chapters of a new romantic novel she couldn't resist buying. Her staff were looking after the boutique, and the children not yet home. Carl had already telephoned to say he'd be a little late tonight, due to a prolonged board meeting – 'But please don't worry, darling. I'll be home as soon as I can.'

'All right, Carl. I'll feed the children first, and then we'll have supper on our own.'

'Good idea. 'Bye, darling.'

''Bye, dear.'

Amanda thought nothing of it. Carl had often been delayed by business meetings. Besides, she still had her butler called Dembrey, inherited from the previous owner of the house. And now she employed an Italian cook, answering to the name of Luigi. He was an artist in that kitchen. No wonder Amanda counted herself a lucky young thing.

As she poured herself another Manzanilla - such an elegant little Spanish wine - she sat back in her favourite fireside wing-chair in the hope of getting into that book before running feet and hungry mouths presented themselves. But the phone rang once more on the small table by her chair. Not Carl again, surely?

'This is Officer Biggs of Paddington Green Police Station, madam. We have your husband, Mr Carl Himmler, here for questioning.'

'Oh my God.'

'Now I don't want you to panic, Mrs Himmler. Everything is under control. But he's been in a slight skirmish in a pub.'

'Oh no.'

'Take it easy, madam. I shall phone you personally in about twenty minutes, and I or one of my colleagues will bring him home after we've had a chat with him. Okay?'

'Okay. And thank you, Officer Biggs. But can you tell me a little more about this?'

'I'll explain all when I or my colleague brings him back. Please keep an ear for the phone.'

'I shall, indeed. I await your call, Officer.'

''Bye for now.'

''Bye, Officer.'

Amanda put down the phone piece, and finished her Manzanilla.

My God. Just as everything in the garden had indeed begun to look rosy. Carl had appeared stable - successful and happy for over a decade. She doted on her two children, Adam and Sally, her boutique was doing well, and... Why did this have to happen?

Hadn't she suffered enough when, barely into her twenties, she lost her elder brother Richard whom she worshipped? He'd had thirteen epileptic fits, one after another, and his young heart gave way. And then her mother was taken from her, struck down from bloody cancer before the age of fifty. Her father grew distant and withdrawn. He associated the loss of his wife and son with England, and he quickly decided America would be his home. But Amanda had stayed to take what life threw at her. The front doorbell rang, and young Adam stood on the step.

'Hi, Mum.'

'Hi, my darling. Have you sung your little heart out?'

'Mum.' The boy stepped into the house, and kissed his mother warmly.

'Seriously, I look forward to hearing your beautiful carols at the Oratory. Any new ones this year?'

'Yes, we're doing one written by Ralph Downes. His own version of 'Adam lay ybounden'.

' Is that why you like it, dear?'

'Well, mum, you named me Adam. And don't worry. I really like my name.'

'Thank you, darling. Oh, here's Sally.'

Adam's young sister Sally had been to a party, and stood excitedly on the doorstep, awaiting her mother's first comments. 'Why, darling, how flushed you look. Have you been drinking?'

'Don't be silly, mummy.' Sally greeted her mother and brother, skipping into the hallway and flopping down on to the sofa in the drawing-room. 'Mummy, you look worried. Has anything happened?' Adam joined his sister in the room to hear what mother had to say.

'Now, you must both be calm, my darlings. Daddy is being questioned by the police.'

'What for, mum?' piped Adam anxiously.

'We don't know, dear. But Police Officer Biggs will be phoning again in a few minutes, and bringing daddy back. So why don't we all relax, and ask Luigi to rustle up a nice meal?'

'Great,' said Adam in unison with his sister.

'Luigi,' called Amanda down the stairs to the kitchen.

'Yes, madam?'

'Can you make something tasty, say Spaghetti Bolognaise for five or six of us, followed by...'

'Apple pie, mum?'

'Apple pie?'

'Sure, Ma'am. Leave it to me.'

'Thanks, Luigi.'

'Is there anything wrong, madam?'

Dembrey had appeared in the doorway of the drawing-room, somewhat flustered and bleary-eyed at the same time.

'Have you been watching 'Dallas Returns', Dembrey? I do sympathize.'

'No, madam. I confess I did drop off in my chair after lunch, and never properly recovered. Please forgive me.'

'You are forgiven, Dembrey.' Amanda's warm smile smoothed the waters. 'I've just spoken to Luigi. Perhaps you will have a word with him now, and ask him to be prepared for a slight delay in serving. He knows what to do.'

'Very good. Will that be all, madam?'

'Yes, thank you, Dembrey.'

With a sweet smile across his wise, craggy face, the butler left the room.

'Mummy, how can you be so calm - when daddy is locked up?'

'He's not locked up, Sally. Merely detained. There's a vast difference.'

'Okay, mummy. Want to hear about the party?'

'Yes.'

Chapter 5

The police interview with Carl had gone quicker than expected, for on the doorstep before Amanda stood an uncharacteristically dishevelled and subdued German industrialist, accompanied by a very calm police officer, ready to talk and advise with equanimity.

'Thank God you're back.' Amanda herself had opened the door to the two men, and Officer Biggs would soon explain the reason for his own presence rather than that of a junior colleague. There had been no need of a further phone call.

'Do come in, officer. Thank you for bringing him home.'

The men stepped inside, and from Amanda's face Adam and Sally took the hint to 'disappear' upstairs for a while.

As the three adults sat in comfortable chairs, Officer Biggs quietly began to expand on the situation. 'This is very serious, Mrs Himmler... No, no, thank you. Just mineral water for me, if you have it.'

Amanda handed the officer a water, and Carl a measure of his favourite brandy to help him regain his equilibrium.

'You see,' continued the officer, 'we have reason to believe there will be an attempt to kidnap either you, Mrs Himmler, or one of your children. Please try to be calm, and let's discuss our strategy for dealing with the matter.'

It was a good twenty minutes before Police Officer Biggs had completed his urgent conference with the Himmlers. Luigi, quite wisely, had delayed cooking the bolognaise until he'd judged it prudent to do so. Moreover, as always, he had cooked a reasonable surplus, not only to satisfy the healthy appetites of the children, but also to accommodate the odd late-comer, whoever he or she might be.

'Well, that all seems clear to me, officer. Would you agree, Carl?'

'Certainly. We will stick together as a family, Amanda, and win through.'

'Good man,' said Officer Biggs. 'What are you going to tell the children, ma'am ?'

'The truth, of course. They are both intelligent youngsters, and well able to keep secrets. I've tested them on several occasions. I think even you would be impressed.'

'Very good.'

'Now, officer, will you stay for a simple meal? Luigi always cooks more than we can eat.'

'That's kind of you, Mrs Himmler, but I must be getting back to the station. I have to make sure my colleagues are one hundred per cent clear on our operation to deal with this matter.'

'I understand.'

'In the meantime, I trust you will endeavour to go about your business and daily lives as normally as possible. Leave the nasty bits to us.'

'Well, we hope it'll never be nasty, for all our sakes, officer.'

'Quite.'

They rose from their chairs, while Carl thanked Officer Biggs for his sympathetic and intelligent handling of the situation, and for the lift home.

As the police officer zoomed off into the London traffic, Amanda closed the front door and prepared to join her family over a belated meal, and...

'Oh Carl. Please don't... Everything will be fine if we stick together.'

Carl dried his eyes, kissed his wife, and called for his children.

Down the stairs ran Adam and Sally, and kissed their father who drew them to his side - just as Dembrey appeared in the doorway... 'Dinner is served, Sir.'

'Thank you, Dembrey. Where is it?' Carl's little quip helped to relieve the tension. They laughed and made for the dining room, while Carl went off to the bathroom for a quick wash and brush-up.

'Heavens, mum. This bolognaise is the best Luigi has ever made.' Adam licked his lips.

'I agree,' joined Sally. 'The sauce is simply...'

'Orgasmic, darling?'

'Not in front of the children, Carl.'

'We know what that means, don't we, Sally?'

'All right, Adam. Tell us after dinner. Let's just discuss what Officer Biggs has told us. But I want your solemn word, Sally and Adam, that you will never talk about it to anyone - until both the police and we as a family are satisfied the matter is behind us.'

Sally and Adam both gave their word to keep secret within the family whatever their mother was about to tell them. 'Good. Now I want you to be very brave, my darlings,' she said.

Carl shot Amanda an express look of concern that she should be careful and gentle in her explanation.

'Don't worry, Carl. They can take it.'

''Course we can, mum. Just tell us.'

'Well, Officer Biggs says the police have reason to believe there will be an attempt to kidnap either me or either of you two children.'

'Gosh, how exciting,' responded young Adam, 'I'll be able to write a real book from first ¬hand experience.'

'I wouldn't like to think you'll ever have to go through that distress - just to write a book, my darling.'

'There are plenty of good novels written from the author's imagination, Adam,' added Carl.

Sally agreed with her father. She had begun to bite her nails with the idea of being kidnapped.

'But why would anyone want to kidnap us, mummy?'

Amanda and Carl explained as simply as they could. They would reserve the intricacies and implications of the threat for another time.

'You see, Sally, both daddy and I earn enough money to tempt a bad person to force one of us to part with a large sum in exchange for your safe return. It's quite simple, really. That's why we want both you and Adam to be extra careful - travelling to and from school, for instance.'

'But I only have a short walk to mine, mum.'

'That's just when a bad person would want you to feel safe, Adam.'

'Without police protection you could be forced into a car, and driven off,' added Carl.

His father's warning was already having an effect upon Adam, who agreed to delay the writing of his novel till his imagination - or experience, if absolutely unavoidable, could do the trick. They laughed again - a welcome break - and got down to discussing an approved taxi-service for Amanda, Sally and Adam, as suggested by Officer Biggs. The driver would be in radio contact with the police who in turn would shadow the vehicle, report on any suspicious cars, stalkers and the like, and be ready to intervene when necessary - with the minimum of fuss.

In the bedroom that night, Carl and Amanda expanded upon the current crisis in their lives. In hushed tones, they quickly covered the possibility of the mafia being involved.

'Which mafia are we talking about, Carl?'

'God knows, Amanda. Every country has its own style. But we Germans are a pretty ruthless lot, too.'

'Don't remind me.'

'And I'm not just talking about the treatment of you Jews in the past.'

Amanda shivered at the thought, and wondered whether Carl could ever turn nasty on her and strike out, as he had done in the pub earlier in the day. She decided to press him gently on that point. 'So tell me how you think today's skirmish began, Carl.'

'Let's talk about it tomorrow, Amanda. You know better than most what a struggle I've had with my aggressive feelings and prejudices - stoked up, perhaps, by a new wave of skinheads. And, to think I was one of them!'

'I remember the photo you showed me, and…'

'But that was ages ago, it seems. I can see now that it's unacceptable behaviour. So you must help me, darling, to expunge it from my life...Come on, let's relax, and... you know.'

Amanda smiled. They kissed, and made ready for lovemaking.

Chapter 6

As the days went by, the Himmlers made their individual adjustments to the new situation. How long the police would remain content with the protection plan or whether or not Carl and Amanda would have to dip into their own pockets, no one would yet say. And whilst Adam and Sally began to enjoy their special status as targets for a kidnap (Adam had changed his mind again about that book of his), Amanda and Carl continued to be concerned for the future. With police resources stretched to the limit, they could not see the arrangement lasting more than a couple of weeks.

Before the first week was out, Carl had grown particularly tetchy. He was supposed to feel grateful to Officer Biggs, but he didn't. His honour was at stake. He decided he would come clean with Amanda over his business, both for his own sanity and for the stability of his marriage. They chose an Italian restaurant in Soho to discuss the situation...

''Um. This liver is delicious.'

'I agree, Carl. As good as we've ever eaten in the world. So tell me what's on your mind. Unload yourself.'

'Well, darling, I don't want you to be alarmed, but I suggested this quiet lunch for a very good reason.'

'Spill.'

'You see, Officer Biggs and I have not been entirely truthful with you because we didn't wish you or the children to become unduly disturbed.'

'You're going all round the bush, Carl. It's not like you.'

'I know, Amanda. Well, it's that the threat to me and therefore to us all as a family comes from a very dangerous part of the world - namely, The Middle East.'

Amanda had already begun to show signs of strain. She felt she could cope with an ordinary threat of kidnap if it were just a matter of money. But a Middle Eastern trap? What was Carl hiding? What was his bloody company up to?

'Now, Amanda. Try to be calm and I'll explain.'

The waiter cracked open another bottle of red, and they held their tongues until he'd gone. But for all their experiences together, their two healthy children, their wonderful sex-life and now this ominous threat looming over them, this could be like their first meeting in Morton's, Berkeley Square on that cold January morning, how long ago was it? The marvellous fact was: they still fancied each other and turned one another on. But sex would have to take that back seat for the moment. Pressing matters of security and a real challenge to their whole way of life had presented itself.

'I shall make it as clear as possible, Amanda. Firstly, the reason for the scuffle in the pub was an irritating insistence from an arms dealer who would not take no for an answer. I had already told the man I'd have nothing to do with his proposal to supply him heavy weapons, let alone nuclear war-heads. My books were full of good, reliable orders from established clients. What need had I to step out of line? I would not do it. Hence the scuffle and fight. My blood had been stirred, and I still regret it, Amanda. It's brought us to this point.' Amanda held Carl's hand and looked at him sympathetically.

'But how are you going to prevent his trying again, or sending someone even more determined?'

'This is the problem, darling. But I can sense something even more insidious.'

'What are you getting at?'

'This may sound incredible to you, but there are dark forces at work, here in London, under our very noses, I believe I shall be relieved of my position as Chairman of our company.'

'You're joking, Carl.' Amanda's face had grown dark with concern and disbelief. 'But why? You're obviously bloody good at your job and make the company millions.'

'Billions, dear, billions'

'So why would they want you out?'

'To save their own skins, I think, is the answer to that. You see, Amanda, nothing is what it seems. The public, thank God, know nothing of what really goes on. For one thing, they'd never believe it; for another, if they did believe it, they'd go mad with a combination of anger, frustration and ultimate helplessness.'

'Yes, my father from time to time tried to explain a few things to me about the wicked world. But like the general public, I didn't believe the stories.'

'There you go, Amanda. I'm not saying the firm would feel the need to kill me. But look what happened to Korborkovsky: Siberia for him, after a show trial.'

'But you don't meddle in politics, Carl. You are strictly a businessman.'

'Not to their minds, darling. Armaments are politics. And then, my short fuse, not to mention my name, makes them feel uncomfortable. And I stick my neck out when I judge it appropriate or just. So there's work to do, darling. I'll need all the support you can give me.'

'You will have it, dear. In fact, I've been thinking of selling the boutique, doing a deal on the designs, and…'

'You don't have to do that, my love.'

'Come on, Carl. We have enough money. We could still manage, despite the world economic situation. This is a serious position you're in. I can see that, now. The children are old enough to cope if we explain things to them. I want to help you.'

'You're an angel.'

'What do you wish me to do?'

'Well, first I want to tell you what is being proposed by the British Prime Minister.'

Amanda's eyes stood out of their sockets.

'You know him that well, Carl?'

'Yes, I do, Amanda. There's quite a bit you have yet to discover about me, darling. Even after all this time. But there are always security considerations.'

'And you sense this is the time to spill a few more beans - now that you have confidence in your wife?'

They looked at one another, and a smile passed across each of their faces. Yes, they trusted one another, but Amanda would still have to give her word...

'You have it, Carl. You know that. My love for you and the children supersedes everything else. Nothing will pass my lips until you give the go-ahead.'

She looked him in the face, and he knew he could trust her with his life.

'Secret One, Amanda: I am to be put on board the elusive nuclear submarine the whereabouts of which the Prime Minister, the Commander of the boat, his Lieutenant and, presumably, the First Sea Lord and few others have knowledge.'

'What's wrong with Siberia? Too common?' She couldn't resist the remarks, and Carl laughed with genuine appreciation.

'Seriously, Amanda, my person on board will be my protection whilst the media will be fed a very different story. They will be told I have been murdered by a Middle Eastern agent. A body will be produced looking much like me. A funeral will take place, with or without you. But this is where I'd prefer your help, darling…'

'Oh, I see. You want me to attend as your widow, dressed in black, with the children suitably solemn, the lessons read, hymns sung, and the whole thing put out on TV for the world to gawp at?'

'Exactly. But you will know the truth, won't you? It will only be for around three months - until the heat is off. What are your thoughts?'

'What about the children, Carl? Are they to be required to play the part of their little lives? Do you really expect them to act this out like professionals?'

'Why not? You're always telling people how clever they are, darling. This is their opportunity to play the biggy.'

At last, Amanda let her imagination fly. Yes, she had to admit she could see young Adam revelling in the idea. Sally might need a little persuasion. But if her brother took up the reins, she'd probably go for it. Besides, the cause would be worth every effort. Her daddy would be safe. And if he did have to change his name...

'And by the way, we will have to change our name. If the Saxe-Coburgs could do it, who am I to argue?'

Amanda's thoughts had coincided with the necessities of life.

'What will you change it to, dear?'

'How about Robert Smythe?'

'H'm. Not bad. A classier Smith, I suppose.'

'There's more, Amanda.'

'Come on, then. I'm all ears.'

'The British Authorities will arrange a new identity. You can either remain my widow, or...' Carl looked into Amanda's eyes with supplication and hope.

'While Carl Himmler rots in his grave, eh? Oh, Carl, this is farcical... But I can see you're deadly serious.'

'I'm afraid so, darling. It's our best chance to begin a new life and put this beastly nonsense behind us for ever. Besides, the money from my estate will go to you and the children, and I'll have to think of something to do with my energy, such as it is.'

'My darling Carl, you've been through so much. If you are willing to relinquish control of your company and marry me as Robert Smythe, who am I to complain?'

Carl was overjoyed with Amanda's decision. They smiled and kissed each other warmly. A few raised eyebrows peppered the restaurant. But what the hell? Carl called for another bottle while Amanda's brain raced on...

'I have an idea. Why don't I approach my father when the time comes - to give you a job in his agency?'

Carl raised his eyes to heaven. 'Or in the theatre, eh? I can just see myself in a Mel Brooks number. I'd love to play piano on stage, dressed in SS uniform. Seriously. When can I start?'

'Carl.' Amanda's face lit up as she rejoiced in Carl's natural humour. If only a few more Germans she knew could fool around like this.

Chapter 7

Without fuss, HMS Astute slipped quietly from her berth at Faslane like an intelligent but lethal killer-whale, in pursuit of her prey. Fully armed, as always, she had on board a very special guest who was about to change his identity for the sake of... How many skins would he really be saving? It took but one fall guy to save many. Whom could he trust, apart from his loving wife and two adoring children?

But he had given his word to the British Prime Minister to abide by the plan. He was paying the penalty for losing his temper in a common London pub, paying the penalty for his unfortunate name which was becoming more than an embarrassment to the other members of the board and to most of the associate companies around the world. He had gone like a lamb to the slaughter, they'd say of him. But what was the alternative? Shameful dismissal as chairman? Shooting by a crude gunman if not by one of his own? Or sly but effective poison in his food or coffee?

The chosen course seemed a good compromise. New name, the regrettable 'murder' of Carl Himmler whose remaining estate would go to Amanda and the children, and the chance to pick up the pieces when things had died down. He was getting to like the idea. If his family played their parts well, he had every confidence a new life with them could be found. Besides, via the approval of the British Prime Minister and German Chancellor, it had been arranged for one half of Carl's current bank balance to be transferred to the bank of his choice under the name of Robert Smythe. The amount would certainly take care of him very nicely for life, should Amanda want out.

'Welcome aboard, Robert.'

The Commander's voice was music to his ears. He had met him a number of times on this very vessel. The respect shone through. Carl's armaments were top quality, but the nuclear nations would not tolerate an unstable chairman of such an important company. One slip was all it took to break the camel's back, and Carl cursed the day he'd entered that London pub with a dodgy arms dealer.

'You look as if you need a drink, my friend.' The Commander handed Robert a healthy dram of Dalwhinnie whisky, and they sat down in the cabin for a private chat.

'Thank you, Commander. You're a gentleman. Cheers, or should I say pro...'

'No need to shout.'

They both burst out laughing. Humour and whisky was just what the doctor ordered.

'I see you're growing a beard, Robert. It suits you. Gives you that...'

'Nautical look?' I suppose it'll be my life for a few months, but I'm sure you'll look after me, sir?'

'You can rely on that. And by the way, you may call me Malcolm for this trip. You're not crew, my dear chap, but a very special guest of Her Majesty's Government.'

'Oh yes, I almost forgot about our beloved PM and the magic he can conjure, just like that, not to mention our circumspect German Chancellor.'

'You've not lost your bite for words, I see. Good man. You may unload your thoughts with me any time you wish, my friend. I am not a cheap spy, nor a lackey for the PM. But he must have his reasons, Robert. You don't mind my calling you by your new name?'

''Course not, Malcolm. I have to get used to it. This is a good way of doing so. You've changed your crew, I've noticed.'

'Thought it best for this trip, old man. Till you're comfortable with your new persona.'

'Good thinking.   I'm feeling better already about all this, thanks to you.'

'Don't mention it. Here, let me top you up.' The Commander poured another dram of whisky into Robert's glass, and re-filled his own. 'Bottoms up, my friend.'

'Bottoms up.' The old Carl Himmler began to smile with the thought of the numerous British phrases assigned to the ceremony of imbibing. They covered such a wide range of emotions, insights and risqué pursuits, no wonder the foreigners liked living here. Mind you, he doubted many would cope with being cooped up in a submarine for more than a day. Wouldn't that be like prison? And wasn't that what Carl Himmler was, after all? A prisoner of Her Majesty?

Back in London, Amanda kept her head, and got on with life without Carl. She had always been strong, thank God, for the whinges of suburban housewives bored her. Besides, she had her hands full, caring for Adam and Sally, to say nothing of the boutique.

As for the covert plan for Carl's 'funeral' and his resurrection as Robert Smythe, the idea positively excited the children. Soon after their intimate lunch in Soho, Carl and Amanda had explained the process of the plan to them as clearly as possible. They had been impressed by the kids' abilities to hold their counsel during the weeks of the police protection scheme. Nevertheless, as before, Amanda extracted from them a solemn promise to keep shtum about the whole affair, for this particular operation would test their skills to the limit. But what interesting lives these children would have.

Leaving aside that book of his, Adam had for some time fancied his chances as an actor. He was as good-looking as most of the child actors he'd seen on TV and in the cinema, and he'd already received a number of accolades from teachers and fellow pupils alike for star and cameo roles in school plays. He was indeed a 'natural'. As for Sally, she went for the intimate, thinking parts of a Dickens play. Yes, she said, she'd go along with her brother in the plot. It would be well worth it for the return of her daddy, with or without a beard.

Carl and Amanda had toyed with the idea of hiding the name of Robert Smythe from the children, but in the end they considered 'in for a penny, in for a pound' the best policy to pursue. It would give Adam and Sally the chance to get used to the notion whilst keeping the presence of their father alive in them. After all, what was in a name? It was the person that mattered.

'Thank you, mum, thank you, dad, for telling us all this,' Adam had beamed, already high on the anticipation of the performance of his life. 'Sally and I will do our very best for you, won't we, Sally?'

'Of course we will, Adam.'

Carl and Amanda had hugged their children tight. They were proud of them. No parents could wish for better kids, and they prayed like mad that all, in the end, would come right, and that their lives would regain their vital stability.

But now daddy was gone, gone from their eyes but not their hearts. They held tight to the hope and trust he would return soon. But first they were obliged to take part in the masquerade of his funeral.

Could they do it? Both Adam and Sally had jumped at the idea initially, in childish bravado and excitement. But could they really be expected to act out this farce for real? With the eyes of the world watching? The media were notorious for prying into people's lives and sparing no one. Not even kids. But they must hold on. They thanked their lucky stars that mummy was with them. She was so brave and cool. What would they do without her?

'Okay, Sally, Adam. Let's have a good meal, then watch something to make us laugh, shall we?'

'Alright, mummy. Why not? We're glad you have another day off from work.'

Amanda smiled on her two children and proceeded to call downstairs to Luigi, while Dembrey laid the dining table. He could sense it was going to be a special night. His antennae had been working overtime recently, with all the comings and goings. Amanda had kept him in the dark since the night of Officer Biggs's visit: she always believed in running a tight ship. It was enough that the immediate family of four should know what was going on. Some mothers would not have told their children. But Adam and Sally had both proved their metal and would, she knew, do so again.

As for her father David, she felt he should be left in peace until it was all over and she had remarried or at least become engaged again. At that point, she might even arrange a quick trip to New York with Robert and the children, and all would be settled.

'We have some fresh calf's liver, today, ma'am. It's beautiful. Shall I cook it for you with wine and sage?' Luigi's culinary enthusiasm could be heard from the kitchen.

'Delicious, Luigi,' answered Amanda whose mouth was beginning to water.

'Spinach and sauté potatoes?'

'Wonderful. Okay, kids?'

'Okay, mummy.'

Chapter 8

While Robert Smythe and Commander Malcolm McGregor relaxed and raised their glasses yet again in expansive conversation covering world politics and international defences, Heads of State, police and secret services were busy putting in place the pieces of an intricate covert operation. Already, the body of a 'murdered' man had been found, slumped upon a bench in Hyde Park, early one morning - just by the Serpentine. The passer-by 'happened' to be an officer of MI6. Coolly, he called Paddington Green Police Station on his mobile, and was put straight through to Police Officer Biggs. Indeed, the call had been expected, and he was told the police would be there in a few moments. A small group of people gathered round the park bench in curiosity and fascination. Who was this elegant man with a rolled-up umbrella, stooping over the body as if he knew what he was doing?

'It's all right,' he said calmly to a persistent bystander who stood too close for comfort, 'I've just phoned the police on my mobile. They'll be here in a jiffy. Don't panic.'

The eyes of the MI6 officer penetrated the face of the onlooker who quickly decided to move on. He was a weak man. The other spectators stood their distance respectfully, and then the police siren could be heard approaching the Serpentine.

Officer Biggs himself climbed from the car with a colleague, and pretended not to recognize the officer from MI6 (he'd known agent Ross for years).

'Good morning, sir. Thank you for your call. So, what have we here?'

'Well, I'd been taking my usual constitutional, and found the poor sod. Thought at first he was a common drunk. But then I realized...'

'Yes, I see what you mean. Okay, constable, I'll help you.'

The small crowd stood back and allowed the 'decencies of death' their proper space. The body of the man was laid in the back of the car, leaving just enough room for the constable.

'Come back with me to the station, will you sir?'

'Of course, officer.'

Agent Ross sat in the front seat of the police car, next to Officer Biggs. The small crowd looked confused as to what was going on. Perhaps they had expected an ambulance to arrive. But Officer Biggs had no time to waste, and the fewer number of people to know about this, the better.

Back in the police station, the serious phone calls began. First the morgue, then the PM, then the papers, and all was set in motion.

TOP GERMAN BUSINESSMAN
MURDERED

stated the DAILY MAIL, next morning in heavy type. 'Could this man Carl Himmler have been a relative of that obnoxious, infamous Heinrich Himmler of The Third Reich? If so, perhaps it was all for the best', continued the editorial. It was uncertain as to whether the editor would be left alone by the controller of political correctness. But it was thought that if an apology was not forthcoming, all the other Himmlers still in the world would be in for a rough ride.

No apology was made, and sensible Englishmen across the world rubbed their hands with glee, happy in the knowledge that England had restored its traditional sense of humour.

The funeral arrangements were made, and Archbishop Nichols agreed to the service taking place in Westminster Cathedral. Saddened though he appeared to be by the sudden death of such a personable character as Carl Himmler, a high profile funeral in his Cathedral, he felt, would bring a further bounty to his parish. For his parishioners had always paid high respect for funerals. It was notable that not a few famous names had graced the Cathedral nave, more at funerals than in the bubbly atmosphere of yet another tying of the proverbial knot.

In deference to the feelings of Carl's widow and her two children, the photographers would not be allowed to take pictures during the service. And their activities afterwards would, it was hoped, be kept on a tight rein. No one knew for certain, even Amanda herself, how the children would cope with the ordeal, when it came to it. Would they break down in uncontrollable tears? Or would they blurt out that the man in the coffin was not their father, but a stooge? They could so easily blow the whole thing and stir up a hornets' nest of which they could have little or no conception. Wisely, Amanda chose not to dwell upon such uncertainties.

The dreaded day had arrived. Black car followed black car. Amanda and the children stepped out of theirs with quiet dignity and poise. Carl's widow looked wonderful, so wonderful that one photograph later gave rise to a few succinct comments in a well-known West End Club...

'I detect a wry smile behind that mask, Gordon.'

'Well, Charles, look at it this way... She's still young, attractive, absolutely loaded, and hardly a silly girl. Get my drift?'

'Who'd take her on, with two kids?'

'I would, given half a chance.'

'H'm.'

Amanda's fears for Adam and Sally mercifully abated as the service and subsequent burial ceremony proceeded. Both children performed like seasoned professionals, and she was proud of them. She could barely wait to take them out to lunch when it was all over. Then they could let go a little, and decide as a close-knit family on their next move.

Amanda was grateful her father could not attend the funeral. She considered his temporary bout of flu to be a blessing in disguise. After all, she had decided not to tell him what was going on. She had given her word to Carl to keep quiet until the coast was clear. Some matters, it seemed, really were for the best.

For their part, Carl's family treated the whole occasion as a sad, genuine funeral. They would keep in touch with Amanda, they said, and offered her and the children an open invitation to Hamburg any time they wished, and for as long as they liked. They would be well looked after.

'Amanda, dear. You must not weep for ever. Carl would not have wanted it. He was a very intelligent man and quite philosophical.'

'I know. And you are right, Marlene. But you must allow me a tiny measure of weakness.'

She hugged Carl's mother who gave Adam and Sally a sweet smile over Amanda's shoulder. The two women held each other in warm embrace, whilst a lone tear trickled down Adam's left cheek. He was indeed an actor, stretching and testing his skills with charm and effect. Sally, by contrast, stood with a glum, pouting posture, spelling danger to anyone observant enough to spot her understandable impatience.

But at last it was over, and Amanda looked forward to that special lunch with the children as soon as she'd heard from... yes, Robert Smythe was the name. She'd book a table at San Marino's, the other side of the park. The restaurant possessed a delightful grotto table where they could all have an intimate conversation. She'd give Luigi and Dembrey another day off, and the house, she hoped, would be nice and quiet when they returned. In the evening they could watch television and go over the plans for their future. They were all quite tired. Much had happened in their lives - squeezed into such a short space of time...

Ah, time... What a fascinating, frustrating concept. If only one could touch it, hold it, make it stand still, go forward or backwards, back so that one could correct those silly mistakes, so that... Amanda checked herself. She was day-dreaming - a rare luxury these days - or was she merely playing God? Now, there's a concept to think about... People either deny HIS existence or think they know who 'HE' is. Only the agnostic gets away scot-free, slipping effortlessly between the nettles of the unbending atheist on the one hand and the actively militant believer on the other.

And the world has suffered enough from the hands of the latter species.

So where were her wistful thoughts leading her? She had to put her trust in someone. She, for one, believed. She just knew Robert Smythe would surface soon. Alive and in good health. And if not, well.., she still had her children.

Chapter 9

She sat in the drawing-room with Adam and Sally, willing the phone to ring... to give her some assurance: the sound of his voice - that rich, smooth voice of security, hope and love. He had been so optimistic, so good-humoured, so solid - like the Rock of Gibraltar. My God, perhaps that's where his submarine might be if she heard from him this morning - old-fashioned style. The landline rang twice before she picked up the phone.

'Oh, sorry. Wrong number.'

'Damn.' Her hand began to shake, but she must keep calm for the children's sake. Another two minutes went by. It felt like hours. And then her new mobile, supplied by Officer Biggs for encrypted speech, gave out its cheerful tones, and she prayed again. Her heart pounded as she stole herself from disappointment...

'This is Robert Smythe here. How are you, darling?'

'Oh, my darling man.' She relaxed with relief and continued. 'Thank you for phoning. I'm fine, now that you've rung. But how are you?'

'Fine, too, thanks. What about the children?'

'They're both well, and here with me now. You should be very proud of them. They came through it all with flying colours.'

Adam and Sally crowded round their mother, and could hardly contain their anxiousness to speak with their father. But first he urged Amanda to remind them he was Robert Smythe...

'I knew I could rely on them. Who's first, darling?'

Amanda handed Adam the mobile, trusting he would give yet another impressive performance and encourage Sally to do the same.

'Hello, Robert. I recognize your voice. Love you, too. Happy you phoned. Yes, yes, I know you have limited time to speak now. Here's Sally.' Adam handed his sister the mobile with a cautionary finger to his mouth.

'Alright, Adam. I know... Hello, Robert. When are we going to see you?'

'Real soon, Sally, dear. I love you.'

'Love you, too, d… Robert.' Sally blushed, but she could be forgiven as she quickly handed back the phone to mummy in embarrassment.

'Me, again, Robert,' said Amanda with a smile. She could hear him chuckling on the other end.

'Now listen, darling. You will be receiving a call from Officer Biggs today. On your mobile. So don't stay around the house unnecessarily. Take the children to lunch, if you like.'

'I had been thinking exactly that, Robert. I'll book a table after this call. Before you go, how long do you imagine you'll be on that boat?'

'About three months, top whack. We're hoping it will only be for two. I'll call you whenever possible. Keep together, darling. I love you, and I just know it'll all work out for us as a family. Keep faith.'

'I do, Robert. You do the same. Love you, too.'

''Bye, darling.'

Amanda put down the phone with a contented sigh, and turned to her children.

'Well, isn't that wonderful, children?'

'Yes, mummy.'

'Where are we going for lunch?' Adam remained practical, though perceptively pleased he'd heard from his father. He was the man about the house now. Dembrey, bless him, was too old for this part. In any case, he'd have to be kept in the dark. 'So dad is the one they kidnapped, eh, mum?'

'Not exactly kidnapped, Adam. This is a little difficult to explain. Let's talk over lunch. I thought we'd go to San Marino, Sussex Place. What d'you think?'

'Great,' responded Adam and Sally together.

They descended the steps of the restaurant and were greeted by the manager, a beaming, charming Italian who plonked a good Latin kiss on Amanda's cheeks plus a cheeky rosebud effort on the lips. Tall and elegant, Michael, the Manager, had always been naughty. She never minded this. She felt comfortable with Italian bravado.

Sally also received a little kiss from Michael, and Adam a gallant, manly handshake which suited him fine.

'Well, Amanda, we've managed to reserve the grotto table for you. Good job you phoned when you did. It's a popular corner for intimate occasions, as you know.'

'Yes indeed, Michael. Thank you.'

The manager ushered his three luncheon guests to the table, and out of earshot of the children whispered: 'My sincere condolences to you, my dear. We read about it in the papers. Enough of my tittle-tattle. I'll send the head waiter across to you straight away. Er.., Raphael. Would you look after my friends, here?'

'Certainly, Michael.'

Over a fine lunch of minestrone soup and lobster salad, they talked about daddy, the future, and the reasons for all the secrecy.

'So you see, Adam, your father is not exactly a common captive. If we all play our cards well, he will be able to join us again, but as Robert Smythe.'

'Will you be marrying him, then, mummy?'

64

'Of course, Sally. Would you like that?'

'Oh, yes.'

'Me, too, mum,' joined young Adam. 'And I'm really going to write that book.' His eyes shone bright. He never imagined he'd get such a chance as this put in his lap. What a story: his own father whisked away, a fake funeral and his expected return as Robert Smythe, Esq. Was mum mad? Did she honestly believe he'd come back? Or was this weird world for real, after all?

'You'll have to change the names, darling. We can't all be Frederick Forsyth.'

'How do you mean, mum?'

'Well, you remember reading 'The Day of the Jackal', don't you?'

'Yes, of course. He gives De Gaulle his real name.'

'So that dates the book, somewhat, and riskily identifies important characters.'

'As in 'The Negotiator'?'

'I didn't know you'd read that, Adam?'

'Yes, and when Margaret Thatcher and President Gorbachev lost power, it made the book seem, how can I say..?'

'It's still a damned good read, darling. But for all our family's sake, I do think you should use other names for your book. Agreed?'

'Agreed. Mum's the word, isn't it, Sally?'

'Yes, Adam.'

'And what is my darling daughter Sally going to do when she leaves school?' Amanda had given her a huge hug and kiss.

'Mummy, I want to be a dress designer, like you.'

'Do you, dear?'

'Look, I've brought some of my sketches with me today.' Sally reached into her school bag and produced some excellent sketches she'd kept secret.

'Sally, they're stunning, darling. I'd no idea you were so good. So this is what you've been up to in that room of yours?'

'Like them, mummy? Really?'

'Like them? They're sensational. I think you should pursue this talent of yours, and I'll give you all the help you need along the way.'

'Oh mummy, you really think they're good? You're not just saying it?'

'No, darling. They're fantastic. Look at them, Adam.'

Adam leant across the table to take a peep. 'Gosh. I agree with mum, Sally. They're great. Really professional. Well done.'

'Thanks, Adam. So, mummy, could I come into business with you?'

'My darling… It's early days for you. You're still at school. Then maybe it'll be university, or…'

'But I could still be a dress designer, couldn't I, in my spare time?'

'Well, yes, I suppose you could, but…'

'Oh mummy, let me come into business with you.'

'Let me think about it, dear. I promise I'll give it serious thought.'

'Thank you, mummy.'

'Now, children, I'm going to pay the bill, and then we'll all go home.'

'May we watch TV, mum? There might be some news about dad. It's all in a good cause.' Adam rolled his eyes.

'Thinking about that book of yours, Adam?' Amanda smiled on her son, and planted a big, proud kiss on his cheek.

Chapter 10

Back at the house, they prepared to relax - come what may - and watch television, including any news coverage on the aftermath of Carl Himmler's demise and burial. They hoped it would not be too painful for them, but they just had to watch and perhaps pick up some clues to the many missing pieces of the jigsaw.

They had scarcely been back half an hour when Amanda's mobile struck up its perky theme. It was Officer Biggs, as expected.

'Hellos madam. I believe Robert Smythe has phoned you today.'

'My word, you are well informed.' Amanda trusted the police officer would not be put off by the note of cynicism in her voice, but she felt entitled to a little more information rather than misinformation from this quarter.

'I'm sorry your husband and I both appear to have misled you, but we wanted to avoid unnecessary strain on you and the children.'

'It has already been quite a strain, I fear. But I imagine your job is a difficult one, to say the least.'

Officer Biggs couldn't agree more, and seemed happy to talk for a while longer.

'The main purpose of my call, madam, is to reassure you of your husband's safety. If you watch the news bulletins tonight, for instance, they could alarm you somewhat. Then there is 'Panorama' later. The whole programme is devoted to the armaments business.'

'How do you know all this, officer?'

'Ah, let's just say I do. Suffice to say I am privileged to know more than the ordinary bobby on the beat. And rest assured your husband - in his new persona, of course, as Robert Smythe - is alive and well, and will return to you and your family in three months' time, if not sooner.'

'Thank you for your assurance, officer. I am most grateful. But may I phone you if I find all this too much to bear?'

'Indeed, you may. But we can do better than that. Would you like me to visit you and the children for a little chat?'

'Most kind. When did you have in mind?'

'Tomorrow morning, say at eleven any good?'

'Perfect.'

'I presume your children have leave from school?'

'Yes, they have, officer.'

'Very good. I think you and I should chat first, if that's possible, and then we'll bring in the children. What are your thoughts?'

'Good thinking. I hope Adam and Sally don't embarrass you in any way. They have, as you can imagine, grown up fast since you and I last met.'

'I'm sure they have. But I understand they performed magnificently at the funeral service. You must be proud of them, Mrs... er...'

'Mrs Smythe soon, perhaps, officer?'

'Indeed, madam. I am, if I may say so, very impressed by your reaction to all this nonsense.'

'Thank you, officer. Perhaps it's not so much a question of nonsense, as manipulation.'

Jesus, maybe Amanda had gone too far. She instantly regretted her words. But they were out. She hoped to God the police officer would appreciate her feelings and understand the touch of bitterness underneath her self-control.

'I can fully understand your anger over this affair, my dear lady, but another purpose for my visit is to give you some insight into the reasons for this clandestine operation. The world, alas, is not what it seems.'

'I know that now, officer, believe me. Nevertheless, I look forward to our chat tomorrow. I hope you'll be able to draw a clearer picture in my mind without, of course, spilling all the beans.'

Officer Biggs laughed. He certainly appreciated Mrs Himmler's intelligence, and made a mental note to try never to insult it.

'Until eleven tomorrow, then?'

'Until eleven. And by the way, could we dispense with these formalities, and use first names? My name is Amanda, and yours, if I may?'

'Certainly. Arthur is the name, and thank you.'

Amanda switched off her mobile and put it down on the coffee table.

'Well, guys?'

'What's with this American expression, mum? Saving time?'

'Don't you approve?'

'It's okay, I guess.'

'That's two Americans for the price of one.'

'All right, mum. I still love you.' And with that, Adam plonked a big kiss on his mother's lips. She gave him a hug, and turned to Sally who appeared anxious to get in on the act.

'Is Officer Biggs really coming to see us tomorrow, mummy?'

'Yes, he is, darling. And I hope you won't be frightened, or anything like that...'

'Frightened? Why should we be frightened? With you to look after us?'

'Thank you, Sally. Now, do we all want some tea or juices before we watch the news?'

It was orange juice for the children.

'Okay, guys, I'll get it,' quipped Adam, grinning at his mother. 'And for you, mum?'

'A cup of Earl Grey, please, darling.'

'Right, I'll do it.'

With their chosen beverages, they all sat back to watch the 6 o'clock news. Adam switched on the set, only to be confronted with a re-run of the funeral. Sally began to weep whilst Amanda reminded her it was not her daddy in that coffin but a...

'Well, I've no idea how they arrange these things, my darlings. It gets a bit confusing at times, I must say.'

'I'm going to find out one day, mum,' announced Adam bravely. 'If I'm to write this book, I've got to do my research.'

'Even if it endangers your own life, Adam?' His mother shot him a hard look for a change.

'All right, mum. I've got the message.'

'Wait till Officer Biggs arrives tomorrow, and you can seek his advice on these matters.'

'What? You mean about dad being kidnapped and told to shut up or else?'

'Adam. What's come over you?'

'I'll tell you, mum. I think we are just pawns on a chess board: sitting ducks for any of them to shoot.'

'And who d'you imagine they to be?'

'The Powers that Be.'

'And who might they be?'

'The Prime Minister, American President, German Chancellor, Russian President...'

'My word, you think big these days, Adam. What about The Monarchy?'

'What about it?'

'They call themselves 'The Firm', you know. And then there's the mafia.'

'Which one?' pressed Adam adroitly.

'Do you know,' responded Amanda keenly, 'that was a question I posed your father after that nasty business in the pub.'

'What was his reply, mum?'

'"God knows".'

Adam laughed, clearly enjoying the banter with his mother. It was all grist to the mill, as far as he was concerned. But Sally had disappeared.

'Where's Sally got to, Adam?'

'I think she got bored with our conversation. She's probably in her room upstairs. Shall I go and find her?'

'There's a good chap.'

After a light supper which Adam and Sally rustled up in order to give their mother a break, they all sat down to watch 'Panorama' on BBC1.

The whole programme, it appeared, dwelt upon the business of Carl Himmler and his company TKH Enterprises, euphemistically listed as though it were merely a firm manufacturing harmless TV satellite dishes. In reality, of course, it produced heavy armaments and components for nuclear weapons, assembling the latter in unspecified locations.

Both Adam and Amanda became more engrossed as the programme continued, for the presenter seemed to be doing a wonderful job in his attempt to enlighten the public on the intricacies and mysteries of the armaments business. It was too much for young Sally to swallow, and she escaped to the privacy of her room, no doubt to work on her designs which had intrigued mummy so much.

The TV presenter carried on: 'Thyssen, Krupp and Himmler are all big names in German history. Carl Himmler, however, whose link with the infamous Heinrich Himmler we have yet to confirm or otherwise, is a relative new-comer to the armaments business, relative in as much as the Krupp arms dynasty goes back as far as 1587. Krupp has been arming Germany for a long, long time. Fritz Thyssen bought out Krupp in 1968, and for the last ten years, the energy injected by the late Carl Himmler has made TKH Enterprises the largest and most powerful conglomerate of its kind in the world. Why then, we may ask, was Carl Himmler dropped? And what led to his pitiful end on a bench in Hyde Park? Was it suicide or murder? Like David Kelly who knew too much about the supposed weapons of mass destruction in Iraq and who had blabbed to the BBC, perhaps Carl Himmler was similarly pushed to the edge of life and took the easy way out. Or did he?'

'My God, Adam. What a life your father is leading. Is this all too much for you, my pet?'

'No, mum. I find it intriguing. But I'm still worried about dad. Why does he have to change his name?'

'It seems it was decided this would be the best course to pursue: a new identity, to pop up as Robert Smythe. And if he comes back to us in good health, Adam, it's better than not at all, don't you agree?'

'Yes, mum. If he comes back.'

'Are you already having doubts? You spoke to him on the phone.'

'Only briefly. And who knows whether this is all to make us feel good? Who knows if Officer Biggs will come here tomorrow to talk to us or shoot us?'

Amanda's face registered horror. What an imagination her young son had. Perhaps her own mind was playing tricks. But the BBC presenter had not finished talking about Carl Himmler...

'We do know he had repeatedly refused to sell to non-bona fide dealers, and that the violent fracas in a London pub last month was the result of one such refusal on his part. One thing is certain: The very name Himmler had begun to look uncomfortable on company headings, and no persuasion from the charismatic Carl could change the board's final decision to dump him. But why such a shabby end to a brilliant career if it was not suicide? The mystery remains unsolved whilst the arms still flow.'

The famous, suitably disturbing music took over to end a memorable broadcast. Not since a similar programme about the business methods of Robert Maxwell a few weeks before his apparent death had the BBC let loose such a gripping 'Panorama'.

'Gosh, mum. What a broadcast. The plot thickens. Is that the expression?'

'Yes, darling. Let's all get to bed. Another big day tomorrow.'

Chapter 11

At eleven o'clock sharp, Officer Biggs stood on the step to Amanda's house and rang the bell.

He was amused to see Dembrey the butler peering demurely round the front door as if the comings and goings of this household were now part of an intricate saga, the mystery of which would for ever elude him. His job, after all, was a comparatively simple one. He had been doing it for years. And as those precious years ebbed away one by one, he could see little point in working himself up into a frenzy. He would leave that pursuit to others. Judging from the special dinner the other night when the mistress and her children had consumed calf's liver and spinach in an atmosphere of nods, half-finished signs and rare winks which left him precluded from the club, he decided that whatever was going on was none of his business and it would behove him to keep out of it.

'Good morning, sir. Can 1 help you?'

'Good morning. Yes, I believe Mrs Himmler is expecting me. Officer Biggs.'

'Oh yes, sir. She did say something about it. Won't you come in?'

'Thank you.'

In stepped the officer, into the elegant house where he'd held his first meeting with the Himmlers just a few weeks ago. For some odd reason, it felt like years. The government, police forces, MI5 and MI6, other Heads of government, not to mention the board of TKH Enterprises had all contributed to a maze of information and purpose brought to a head in a simple production of a body, a funeral, the placing on board a nuclear submarine of an important civilian, news coverage, new identity - and 'Bob's Your Uncle'. Job done. If only all life could be that easy. Only joking, he told himself.

And for another strange reason, the experienced Arthur Biggs felt as though he were about to step into a clever mouse trap and that he was the mouse rather than the diplomatic Special Branch Officer in charge of operations. That Amanda Himmler was bright, he had no doubt. And her children, by all accounts, particularly the boy, were beyond their years and able to pick up on any exposed weaknesses within their sights. Before he had time to shake off these thoughts, he was confronted by Amanda.

'Good morning, Arthur. How are you?'

'Good morning, mad... I mean, Amanda.'

'We agreed, didn't we?'

'Of course.'

'Do come into the drawing-room, Arthur. The children are upstairs in their rooms. So we'll call them when we're ready, shall we?'

'Very good.'

'Would you care for a drink? Something stronger than mineral water, or coffee..?'

'Coffee with milk would be fine. Thank you.'

'Dembrey. Would you bring a coffee with milk for the officer, and black coffee for me?'

'Very good, madam.'

Dembrey left the room with a smile. He'd see out his days peacefully, he hoped.

Amanda had always treated him well. She was quite different to the previous, aristocratic boss (also a woman) but kind and intelligent, nevertheless. He would serve her as best he could, now that there was no Mr Himmler around, apart from young Adam, of course. He'd have to watch him.

So where had the young master been this morning? He said he was going to buy a newspaper at Knightsbridge Tube Station. He said nothing about popping into the local police station to check up on Officer Biggs. But that's what the cheeky young puppy had done.

As they drank coffee and nibbled on the odd biscuit or two, Officer Biggs expanded upon the scenario in which Carl, Amanda and the children had found themselves. The Officer could not emphasize enough the importance of accepting life rather than death. This was not a threat. It was simply a case of Carl either facing a sticky end at some point when he was not looking or settling for a completely new identity, re-uniting with his loving family, and living out a happy life till the good Lord took him.

'Yes, I can see that, Arthur. But I can't understand why TKH Enterprises should rid themselves of a man who has, by all accounts, built the company up to become the biggest and best?'

'Good question, Amanda. I know Carl was no politician, but as far as a few characters in his company were concerned, he might just as well have been one. For them, as for others, he was becoming too successful, too powerful, too dictatorial, and with a bit of a short fuse…'

'All right, Arthur. No need to go on. I can see the picture. But can we be sure Carl will turn up again as Robert Smythe - unharmed, healthy and willing to begin a new life with his family? For our part, we, and that means Adam, Sally and I myself are willing to start again as the Smythe family.'

'That's wonderful, Amanda I'm very happy you've all come to that decision. Shall we call in the children?'

'Yes, let's do that.' Amanda went out into the hallway, and called upstairs to her children.

'Okay, mummy. We'll be down.' Down the stairs romped the children, and entered the drawing-room with bright, alert faces.

'My word, Amanda. What handsome children you have… Adam…' Officer Biggs held out his hand to Adam who shook it firmly and with great dignity. The officer was very impressed. Sally almost curtsied and shook hands with the powerfully built guest who had come to see mummy and explain things that were difficult to understand.

'I hear, Adam,' began Officer Biggs without warning, 'you have been to the local police station this morning to check me out.'

A look of horror crossed Adam's face. He didn't expect this, but then he was but a boy and as yet inexperienced in the ways of the world. Nor did he have knowledge of police procedure and current organization. Officer Biggs was indeed a big noise. Paddington Green Police Station may sound a bit like 'Dickson of Dock Green' to some minds, but it was and is anything but. Heading high security and the Anti-Terrorist Unit, Biggs himself had previously worked at Scotland Yard and had personal and professional contacts with MI5 and M16 to say nothing of The Prime Minister. Oh yes, he was the business all right, and young Adam began to eat humble pie. Officer Biggs looked kindly on the boy...

'You were only doing what you thought best in the circumstances. I would have done the same at your age, and especially if I'd been asked to swallow a farcical story of my dad's change of identity.'

'Thank you, officer.'

'Except, son.., it happens to be true. He is changing his identity so as to be with you again as your father. Okay?'

'Okay, officer. It's just that when my father told me about this, I didn't quite believe him. It seems too...'

'Far-fetched?'

'Yes.'

'But life is stranger than fiction, as they say, Adam, and no novel can equal life as it really is.'

'Except mine, officer.'

'Oh?'

'Yes, Arthur. I meant to tell you. Adam is writing a novel.'

'Is he indeed? Well, you have plenty of material, my lad, haven't you?'

'I have.' Adam gave Officer Biggs an old-fashioned look which brought an appreciative smile to the policeman's face.

'What about my designs, mummy?' piped Sally. She had no intention of being left out.

'Yes, dear. And Sally is working on some beautiful designs. I think she'll outclass her own mother one day, Arthur.'

Smiles broke out across the room as Sally proceeded to show 'uncle' Arthur what she had been doing all this time.

Chapter 12

Good. The Himmlers, destined to become The Smythes as soon as Amanda had re-married the 'resurrected' Carl, had settled for the compromise. Arthur Biggs's job was difficult enough without intelligent, honest citizens delving too deeply into the muddy waters of the controlling powers.

Officer Biggs was one of those links between the secret services, government and the police which was accessible to the public. And his status, experience and knowledge was such that his work was seen as invaluable to 'The Establishment'. Given the importance of the Himmler affair in terms of world security and diplomatic sensitivities, it was thought by the Prime Minister that Arthur Biggs would be the best man to see the case through and wrapped up with the minimum fall-out. There had been too many nail-biting moments for the PM along the way for this one to go wrong. Even Biggs hoped the recent meeting with Amanda and the children would be a one-off occurrence.

As soon as he had returned to Paddington Green from Brompton Square, he telephoned the PM on his special line.

'Good to hear from you, Arthur. How did it go?'

'Better than I'd anticipated, Prime Minister. There were a few touchy moments with Amanda and that bright young son of hers, but...'

'You handled it, eh? Yes, I'd heard about Adam Himmler from another source. Carl used to take him around the world a bit whenever possible.'

'That's right, sir. Anyway, I think we can be satisfied everything has worked out well - so far.'

'Very good. And I thank you, Arthur, for your intelligent handling of this matter.'

'Thank you, Prime Minister. Glad to be of service.'

'I think in the light of the family's acceptance of the new identity of our friend on the sub, we might arrange for him to be let loose a month earlier than proposed. What do you say?'

'Why not, sir? He's unlikely to step out of line now, and I know Amanda and the kids will be over the moon with joy. She's an intelligent woman, Prime Minister. I am one hundred per cent sure she can be trusted to keep her head down.'

Arthur Biggs omitted to mention young Adam's naughty visit to the local police station. There was no point in stirring up a hornets' nest, now that he'd come this far in the case. Adam had appeared to accept Officer Biggs's high status and had bitten the bullet with good grace.

'Very good, Arthur. I shall contact Commander McGregor, and you, presumably, will inform

Amanda her man will be released a month earlier than we'd thought likely. But please reiterate the need for caution in her life-style. She should continue to mourn for a little longer.'

Arthur Biggs joined the PM in a chuckle. After all, there was always a funny side to a tragedy, apparent or not.

'And what about living arrangements, Prime Minister?' continued Officer Biggs. 'Don't you think they should live apart for a few months before they meet by chance, fall in love, and..?'

'Re-marry? I agree, Arthur. Talk with Amanda about this. May I leave this delicacy with you?'

'You may indeed, Prime Minister. Nice to speak with you again. All the best, sir.'

'And to you, Arthur. Keep in touch.'

'I will, sir. 'Bye.'

'Good news, Amanda. It's Arthur Biggs, here.'

Amanda was taken aback by the officer's overt cheerfulness. Not that he'd ever been miserable in her presence or on the phone. Nevertheless, she sensed a change of gear in his disposition.

'Hello, Arthur. What is the good news?'

'Robert will be released a month earlier than planned, so that means…'

'Around the middle of March?'

'Absolutely. Happy?'

'I should say so, Arthur. How did you manage it, or shouldn't I ask?'

'Shouldn't ask, my dear lady.'

'Will you inform Robert of this?'

'The Prime Minister will be contacting the Commander of the submarine, and no doubt you will be hearing from Robert very shortly.'

'Well, Arthur, I do thank you for your work and attention to this matter. I still feel funny about the whole affair, as you can imagine, but you have given me a sufficient inkling of the ways of this wicked world to persuade me it's always better not to rock the boat. Literally, in this case?'

'A wise conclusion, Amanda. If I may give an example of an exceedingly rich man rocking the boat and subsequently spending unwelcome time in Siberia... Perhaps you can guess the man to whom I refer?'

'Oh yes. Korborkovsky, you mean?'

'That's the man. If he hadn't meddled with politics, Putin would have let him keep his money. And as I've indicated before, Amanda, Carl Himmler was seen by more than a few of his fellow directors, not to mention Heads of certain governments, to be on the brink of stepping outside his sphere of pure business. Let's leave it at that for the moment, shall we, Amanda?'

'Agreed, Arthur. I am more than happy Robert is coming back. And I assure you I shall do my best to be discreet.'

'I am happy to hear that.'

'And in line with my discretion, I propose he and I should live apart for a few months. It will look more natural that we meet casually in a bar or restaurant. What are your thoughts..?'

Officer Biggs couldn't believe his luck. This job was proving to be a doddle for him: such a change from the frustrations of getting known criminals and terrorists behind bars...

'Exactly yours, would you believe? I understand Robert has put on a little weight since he's been on the sub, and his beard looks quite impressive. So you'll have a new man, Amanda.'

'I don't need a new man, Arthur, but I take your point. Can't wait to tell the children.'

'Give them my kind regards, won't you?'

'I shall, and thank you again. You'll keep me posted?'

'I will. And listen out for Robert's call.'

'That's for sure.'

Officer Biggs put down his phone piece, and turned his attention to a normal business line. Not that any of his work could ever be called normal. The anti-terrorist unit which he controlled had stacks of false trails and more than a few suspects. But when he did have these people in his grasp, far too often his hands were tied by an over-zealous pursuit of human rights, and the terrorists would slip from his fingers. Compounding this was the constant flow of suicide bombings, ensuring no policeman could rest on his or her laurels.

It would not be long before Arthur Biggs reached retirement age. Would he be in line for a Knighthood, he wondered, now that he was about to wind up one of the most delicate clandestine cases of his career? He'd long fancied plonking his bum down on one of those fancy leather benches in The House of Lords, and then standing up to spout his head off in his own, measured time. He'd never forgotten Harold Macmillan's maiden speech soon after he'd been dubbed The Earl of Stockton. It was all about ''selling the family silver''...

Arthur fondly recalled The Earl's avuncular, clever dig at Mrs Thatcher and her policy of privatizing everything, no matter whether it made sense or not. He, Lord Biggs, could give 'em a run for their money. Of that, there seemed little doubt. But would he ever be capable of such a smooth delivery as Macmillan and his ilk? He had had too many years of hard graft, dealing with violent criminals, IRA suspects, and nowadays wave after wave of Islamic fundamentalists, ever determined to overthrow Western civilization.

But as soon as the Himmler case was wound up, he'd seek early retirement - whether he was in line for The Lords or not. Nevertheless, he still had hopes the PM would consider the Himmler case the pinnacle of Arthur's career and offer him that peerage.

Chapter 13

Amanda's mobile chimed again, and Robert Smythe could be heard on the other end of the line.

'Robert, you sound in fine spirits. No doubt you've heard the good news?'

'Oh yes, darling. The Commander gave me the thumbs up this morning. But in our cosy discussions over a glass or two, he's convinced me of the need for great discretion on all our parts. Living arrangements, for a start. What are your ideas?'

'I think we should live apart until our marriage, dear. Too many eyes, ears and tongues in central London, right now. Do you agree?'

'Well, we could, I suppose, buy a 'safe house', say in Barnes or Chelsea. They're used to seeing arty types come and go. My beard, for instance, lends just that touch of unkemptness to which I have long aspired.'

Amanda laughed. She knew damn well Carl Himmler wouldn't have been seen dead hanging around the cafes and bars on the riverside, let alone a seedy piano bar in Chelsea. But necessity is the mother of invention, and Amanda had always been practical. Besides, before meeting Carl Himmler, she was known to be quick off the mark when it came to men - whether they looked like businessmen or artists - just so long as they had what it takes, and that included a brain as well as a body.

'A Hippy we will be, then, Robert?'

'Not entirely, darling. There are limits. I think I shall trim my beard to look like a successful Hollywood actor on vacation. What d'you think?'

''Um. Very nice. Robert Redford look-alike, Brad Pitt, Tom Cruise... Oh, there's so much choice.'

Robert laughed and joked: 'After all, if your father can get me the part, I'm bloody sure I could play it.'

'I'm sure you could, darling. But one thing at a time. Let's work out our plan for a safe, smooth run-up to my new marriage to a Mr Smythe.'

'Good thinking, Amanda. I knew you weren't just a pretty face.'

'No need to exaggerate, darling.'

'How could I be exaggerating when I'm talking about you? God, I miss you, Amanda.'

'I miss you, too, darling. But it won't be long now. So what do we do, seriously? Buy a house in the country, and meet there?'

'Not a bad idea, Amanda. It did cross my mind. Safer, probably, than anywhere in London. We could meet on weekends. Put your manageress in the boutique on Saturdays.'

'Yes, I could. She's covered me these last few weeks. Often suggesting she should take more responsibility - especially after Carl's sudden death.'

'Ah yes, what a loss that must be to you, darling. But we are mature people. Life goes on, and there's always me to fall back on.'

They both chuckled, enjoying the new game they were obliged to play. They hoped to God it would all be worth it. Then, perhaps, they could cease acting, and be themselves.

'Come to think of it,' he continued, 'Robert Smythe does have a nicer ring than Carl Himmler, don't you agree?'

'Well, I must say,' responded Amanda, 'for me it has less of a menacing memory.'

'I know just what you mean. Heinrich Himmler was a loathsome man. Such evil in him... But let's talk about more pleasant matters.'

'Yes, let's. Okay, Robert. I'll get my skates on and look for a decent property in the country - a place we can all enjoy. Leave it to me.'

'Thank you, darling. How are the children?'

'They're both fine: out at the moment. I've told them to be very careful. Adam, by the way, is really becoming the little man about the place. Looks after his mother, bless him.'

'I'm very proud of him, Amanda. Please give them both my love.'

'I will.'

'Phone you over the weekend. Happy hunting.'

'Thanks, dear. 'Bye.'

''Bye, darling.'

Amanda switched off and held her mobile in her hand for a while. She pondered on the hype this invention had generated - even among the so-called deprived nations of the world, nations that had for too long suffered at the hands of brutal dictators but had suddenly blossomed and run wild with understandable excitement. The mobile had become a dubious status symbol, brashly used in restaurants with its irritating popular tunes or synthesized 'funky' rhythms. They had all got in on it: even the powerful Siemens had succumbed. German it might remain, but could it really be expected to exude with a snatch of one of the Brandenburg Concertos? Amanda made a mental note to ask Motorola to give Bach a boost. As she mused on these thoughts, her landline rang loud and clear.

'Hello, Amanda. Have you heard from Robert?'

'Yes, I have, Arthur. He's in good spirits and very positive as to the future.'

'Good. I'm very happy for you both. Have you decided on where he might live? No need to tell me the exact address. I'm not prying into your lives for ever, believe me.'

Amanda's mind was racing. Could she really believe Officer Biggs - after all that had happened? If he was involved in the cover up or clandestine operation as he preferred to describe it, why should he want to give up on its result? Would he not be interested in the new lives of

92

Robert and Amanda Smythe? If he knew the Prime Minister that well, and had connections with MI5 and MI6 as he had indicated, would he not himself be a marked man? They would expect him to follow up the aftermath of the case, at least until his retirement. And maybe beyond. For what better or more elegant cover could there be for a Peer of the Realm to remain a fountain of all knowledge?

'I don't view you as a prying man, Arthur. You have your job to do. No, we have not yet decided. Probably outside London, I should say.'

'Good idea, Amanda. Somewhere quiet, I think, will be best. And I want you to know I am always at your service. Please feel free to contact me should you ever be threatened or sense danger.'

'Thank you, Arthur. I appreciate that offer. Who knows what might happen in the future? The future's not ours to see, as the song goes, eh? Que sera, sera.'

'Quite.'

What a conversation. As Amanda replaced the receiver, her mind continued to buzz. She felt she had already become the amateur detective. She'd long admired the part of Miss Marples on television. Not that Amanda would find the time to delve into the twists and turns of all these Agatha Christie stories. By God, she was living out a more dramatic story herself. And did she have to be a 'sitting duck' as her young son Adam had described the scenario? Yet even Adam had been put in his place rather smartly by Officer Biggs who had not shot the family as Adam had feared. Moreover, her conversations with Robert were becoming more upbeat with each call. Surely a common captive would never sound that content if his arm were being twisted? There would be some give away in the voice, some tell-tale intonation that only a close friend or wife could detect.

No, when all was said and done, despite the obvious frustrations of the separation, the mock funeral and the obligation to a change of name from Himmler to the agreed Smythe, Amanda held close to the belief in her man's reappearance and a new life with the children as the Smythe family.

The front bell rang, and Dembrey answered the door. In bounced Sally with a bunch of flowers for mummy. Adam followed, hungry as usual... 'Hi, Mum. What's for tea?'

'Kippers.'

'Mum, don't tease.'

'Listen, children. Daddy is coming back in March. Happy?'

Chapter 14

Adam and Sally were overjoyed to hear of their father's impending release. What would he look like? They knew about his beard, but would he have grey hair with all the worry he'd endured? Mum was even showing signs of a few grey hairs. But she had so many gorgeous colours in her mop, that it all seemed to blend into a mosaic of delight. She was a fine-looking woman, and she was their mum.

As far as Amanda was concerned, the wait for Robert's release would undoubtedly be more frustrating were it not for the rush to find the right house in the country. She had always possessed good instincts for position, feel of a property and value for money. Not that money was a problem. She counted her blessings on that score. But the fact remained: her taste was refined, subtle and individual.

Luckily, the market remained awash with attractive properties, and within the week Amanda had spotted an unusual, old and secluded house, tucked in off a lane – a stone's throw from Woodstock in Oxfordshire. From the pictures, it looked perfect: a well-proportioned, sixteenth century manor which had passed through several interesting hands, including an eccentric academic of Oxford University. The advertisement suggested a complete restoration. But it was quite habitable. Amanda phoned the agent, and an appointment was made for a viewing the following day.

'Would you like to come with me, my darlings?'

''Course we would, mum.'

'Are we coming back here the same day, mummy?'

'No, Sally. I think we'll stay overnight at 'The Bear' in Woodstock - if they're not fully booked.'

'Is that a pub, mum?'

'A very nice pub, Adam. Or old inn, I should say. You'll like it. Excellent food.'

Adam licked his lips. He was all set to go.

'Great. Will we have time to look around Oxford while we're there?'

'We'll see, dear. The first thing is to view the house and perhaps another one in the area. I want it to be comfortable for daddy. He will be staying there until I marry him.' Amanda shot Adam an old-fashioned look of amusement. She seemed to be enjoying acting out this farce. But then, Adam fancied his chances, too. Sally was content to go along with the game - as long as it brought back her daddy.

They motored along an old route in their 4 by 4, on to the A40, through High Wycombe, Buckingham, and on to Headington and then Oxford. Amanda headed for the agent's shop in the town centre. They were lucky in finding a parking space so near to it. Someone in the sky just had to be in a good mood.

A Mr Reid welcomed them and seated them in comfortable chairs. But Amanda remained conscious of a ticking clock, and produced her business card.

'Ah yes, Miss Amanda. My wife has bought some of your lovely dresses. She'd be delighted I've met you. I imagine you have limited time, so perhaps we should make straight for the manor which interests you, and take a couple more property details with us. What do you say?'

'Let's do that, Mr Reid. Ready, children?' 'I suggest we take our car, Mr Reid. We can all get in the 4 by 4, and we'll run you back here, after we've taken a look.'

'All right, madam.'

'Amanda will do nicely. And your name, if I may?'

'David, at your service. Pleased to meet you, Amanda.'

'Likewise. Ah yes, this manor appears just up my street, so to speak.' Amanda glanced again at the photos and details of the property that had taken her fancy.

'Needs a bit of work to bring it up to scratch, I'd say. But I think you'll still find it comfortable. And very atmospheric.'

'Has it got a ghost, Mr Reid?'

'Several, 1 believe, young lady. But don't take my word for it.' David Reid grinned through his ill-assorted set of dentures. His impression of Dracula made Sally laugh.

'Okay, folks. Let's go.'

Into the 4 by 4 they all piled, and motored towards Woodstock. In remarkably short time they were approaching the wall surrounding the house. Amanda pulled up in the nearby lane, and down they climbed and walked through the front gardens, neatly laid out before the manor. As they approached the house which stood expectantly before them, the family felt as though they had been here before, as if they had owned it in a past life. The house seemed to call out to them, to the Himmlers and soon to become the Smythes, to take it on and care for it, to restore it to its former glory.

As they climbed the steps, Mr Reid produced his key to unlock the front door. They entered with quiet respect so as to soak up the atmosphere with maximum effect. Sally soon claimed she had seen her first ghost - that of an elegant lady in a beautiful dress, smiling at her on the staircase. As the lady vanished, Sally giggled with delight. She would never again fear apparitions, she exclaimed.

They had reached The Long Gallery, and Amanda glimpsed a young girl practising the harpsichord. The girl turned her head and gave Amanda a wonderful smile as if to say: 'We will do you no harm. You'll love this house.' As the image vanished, Amanda found herself smiling, too. Not a trace of fear could she feel, but a warm, loving glow which enveloped her being and pointed the way. She was hooked.

Adam, strangely, had no such luck, but he had hopes - 'I expect my experience will be more dramatic. Hope it won't be bad.'

'Of course it won't, Adam. Think good thoughts, and everything will be fine.'

When they had completed their inspection of the house and grounds, Amanda turned her attention to the children. 'Well, what d'you think, both of you?'

'Love it, mummy.'

'Ah yes, mum. Let's go for it.'

'Well, David.' Amanda faced the agent with a humorous expression on her face. 'You've heard the children's verdict. May I make an offer? It will be a firm one. Cash if preferred.'

'Of course, Amanda. I'm sure it will be accepted if it's reasonable. What did you have in mind?'

The mouths of Adam and Sally opened wide as their mother coolly announced her offer. Mr Reid appeared to stand his ground, and maintained commendable self-control, for he knew he was dealing with another professional. So what? Amanda was used to doing deals, and she had invariably hit the nail on the head. As regards this one-off house, however, could she be about to fall over the edge?

'Allow me to ring the owner on my mobile, Amanda.'

'Go ahead, David.'

Two minutes went by, but for the children it felt like two hours.

'Please, please don't let mummy lose the deal. We love this house. Please God, let mummy have the house...'

'All right, Amanda. Your offer has been accepted. Congratulations.'

The children couldn't believe it. Their mum had done it again. She was a wizard, if ever there were one. And even if Adam's ghost turned out to be a bit of a shyster, he was darned sure his mum would deal with that, too. In any case, his writing would come on leaps and bounds. This house might just be the catalyst to his success...

'Mum, may I give you a kiss?' Adam leapt up to his mother's face and plonked a healthy one on her lips.

'Why Adam, thank you darling.'

'And one from me, mummy?' Sally would never be excluded.

Amanda happily drove David Reid back to his office in Oxford. She had no desire to look over other properties, now. She would put down her deposit on the manor house, and then drive back towards Woodstock, have lunch with the children at The Trout on the way, and check in at The Bear early evening. It would be a day to remember.

'Gosh, mum,' said young Adam after Amanda had done the deed on the house, 'you've actually put down a deposit on the manor. I didn't know it could be done that quickly.'

'It can if one has the money, darling. And the determination. Of course, not everyone has a nose for property. You'll see when you get older.'

Adam smiled, and looked on his mother with love and satisfaction. If he inherited half her skills, he'd be a happy young man.

'Why is it called The Trout Inn, mummy?' Sally wasn't too sure whether she'd like trout for lunch.

'You don't have to have trout for lunch, darling. It's called that name because there are trout swimming in the river, just beside the old inn. And there are peacocks in the garden.

'Sounds lovely.'

'It is lovely, Sally. After lunch, we'll drive to The Bear and check in - before it gets dark. You'll be sharing a room with Adam, dear. Is that all right?'

'Of course it is, mummy. And if I see a ghost, maybe Adam will see it, too.'

'All right, darling. That's enough about ghosts.'

Chapter 15

Over dinner at The Bear, Amanda promised that before returning to London, she'd take the children around Oxford. At least Adam would find it interesting.

'Oh, great. That's where most of the Prime Ministers studied, wasn't it, mum?'

'Not just Prime Ministers, but great writers and philosophers, Adam. And where do you imagine most of our famous spies went?'

'Cambridge.'

'Spot on. Makes you wonder, doesn't it?'

'I spy with my little eye...' began Sally with enthusiasm.

'We're not talking about ghosts, Sally, but people who undermine the security of their own country. Traitors. Treacherous ghosts, if you like.'

Adam's remarks took Amanda by surprise. Her son was even brighter than she'd suspected.

'Where did you learn the meaning of the word 'undermine'?' She gave Adam a quizzical glance and added: 'From a dictionary or..?'

'From dad, actually. You remember when he took me on that trip to Moscow, last year?'

'Oh yes. You told me you found it strange but intriguing.'

'But it's too cold for me, mum. Anyway, dad pointed out the flat where Guy Burgess stayed, and we went on talking about spies and then politics in general.'

'My word, Adam, you seem to have lived a full life already. I wonder what the next twelve years will bring?' Amanda gave her son a big hug. Then, of course, there was another; for Sally. 'Okay, children. Up to bed, now. Sleep well. I shall just have a night-cap with the landlord, and then I'll follow you.'

'All right, mummy. Goodnight.'

'Goodnight, mum.'

'Goodnight, my darlings.'

Next morning, Sally woke early and knocked on her mother's door.

'Good morning, dear. Come and give mummy a kiss.' Sally toddled over to the bed and kissed her mother affectionately. She sat on the bed excitedly. 'Don't tell me you've seen another ghost?' Amanda was getting worried about Sally.

'No, mummy. Nor has Adam. Perhaps ghosts don't like The Bear. But I like it. It's fun. Lovely meal last night.'

'Yes, it was delicious, wasn't it? We'll have breakfast downstairs at 8.30, if Mr Brewster is kind enough to lay it on for us. He's a good landlord: known him for years.'

'Then we go into Oxford?'

'That's right, darling. Wouldn't it be funny if one of you two children went there to study?'

'Yes, mummy. But you know I want to be a fashion designer. I don't have to go to university for that, do I? You didn't.'

'You're quite right, dear. But... Well, we'll see. Oh, this looks like Adam, all spruced up.'

Adam walked into the room. He had already washed and dressed. He would act the proper little man. He strolled across to the bed and gave his mother a gallant kiss. 'Thank you, Adam. Looking forward to seeing the colleges?'

'Yes, mum. Wouldn't it be great if I became a famous writer before studying at Oxford?' Amanda studied her son's face with enthusiasm.

'So you'd really like to go there, darling? What would you read for your degree?' A silence prevailed, and Amanda wondered whether her son properly understood the question or simply did not appreciate the terminology and finer points of the academic system. But he obliged with a reverent bow of his young head: 'History.'

'Do you know, that's what my own father is always on about, Adam. "If you kids were taught a bit of history", and so on. He's right, of course. We'd all better understand the present if we studied the past.'

'And the future will depend on what we've learned and what we do now, mum.'

'That's right, darling. Good thinking. Unfortunately, most of us are only concerned with living for the moment. I know that's a valid viewpoint, especially for young people. But if one is a thinker like you, it's not good enough, is it?'

'No, it isn't, mum. So you do understand me?'

''Course I do, Adam. And I hope I understand my Sally, here.' Amanda drew her daughter closer to her and kissed her. 'Now, my darlings,' she continued, 'let mummy get up and shower. Why don't you two go downstairs and begin your breakfast?'

'But we'll have breakfast with you, mum. Come on, Sally. Let's go downstairs and look around the place. I'm sure Mr Brewster won't mind.'

'Okay, children. Now, be on your best behaviour.'

''Course we will, mum.'

Eventually, they found a parking space in Oxford, a lucky slot opposite St.John's College. As they climbed out of the 4 by 4, Amanda pointed across to the college and quizzed Adam. Which Prime Minister do you imagine went there as a student?'

'I'm afraid I don't know, mum. Who?'

'Tony Blair.'

'Remind me not to go there.'

Amanda laughed but had not finished. 'He was a very bright boy, Adam,' she admonished, 'whatever some of us thought of him as a Prime Minister.'

'Where did Mrs Thatcher go, mummy?' Sally was determined to edge into the conversation.

'Somerville, I think, darling. But now we're here, do you want to look around St.John's or move on until we feel drawn to a particular place?'

'Let's move on, mum.'

They walked past St.Giles, and turned left into Broad Street towards The Sheldonian.

'That's where my uncle Tom received his BA and MA from the Vice Chancellor in traditional ceremonies, Adam.'

Amanda pointed out the famous old buiding along the street.

'Really, mum? What was his subject?'

'Modern languages. Got a BA First Class Honours. Brilliant man, as I recall.'

'May we look around his old college, for fun?'

'Why not? It was Lincoln - just here, in Turl Street.'

They turned right into The Turl (as it's known by the undergraduates), and walked along towards Lincoln College, passing Jesus on the right and Exeter on the left. Lincoln was the next one along, adjoining Exeter. There was a small group of animated visitors, cluttering the front porch, but Amanda and the children politely negotiated themselves into the front quadrangle.

'What a pretty little square, mummy,' exclaimed Sally, awed by the fact her mother's uncle spent time here, how many moons ago?

'It's called a quadrangle, Sally. And I agree. It's very sweet, and beautifully kept.'

'Who's statue is that, tucked in the niche in the wall, mum?'

'That's John Wesley. He was a Fellow of this college, and founded The Methodist Movement.'

'Oh.'

'Why just 'oh'?' Amanda shot Adam a curious look of challenge.

'Well, it's only a breakaway from The Church of England, isn't it?'

'You could say The Church of England is a breakaway from the true Catholic Church.' Amanda's curious look prevailed, and her son appeared to be enjoying the challenge. 'And then again,' continued Amanda, 'your own mother converted to Catholicism from Judaism, didn't she?' Amanda softened her look into a warm smile.

'Wasn't that to make it all square with dad, so you could marry?'

'Sometimes, Adam, it's the other way round: the Gentile converts to Judaism. But in my case, my love for your father propelled me into rethinking an honest position regarding my faith.

There are more wars and suffering over religion than anything else. Think about it.'

Before Adam could respond to his mother's thesis, Sally broke into the conversation with an anxious question. 'Oh mummy, why is daddy in prison?'

'He's not exactly in prison, darling. Adam, we'll resume this discussion later. (Adam nodded his agreement) Not prison, Sally. He is being kept safe from anyone who'd want to harm him.'

'But who'd want to harm daddy? He's a nice man.'

Amanda smiled. 'I know, darling. It's all a bit difficult to explain to you right now. Just rest assured he's safe and well, and will come back to us very soon. That's why mummy is going to buy the manor you like so much. All right?'

'All right, mummy. I'll try to save my questions until daddy comes back, and...'

'And then,' joined Adam, 'you probably won't have any. We'll all be over the moon with joy.'

Just then, Amanda's mobile buzzed its little theme...'This is your spirit guide speaking.' It was Robert, up to his pranks again, but he seemed in fine shape. 'Seriously, darling, I shall be back on the 15th of March. It's all fixed.'

'Oh, wonderful, Robert. Wonderful news. Now I have some for you. I've put down a deposit on a lovely sixteenth century manor, just outside Oxford. We're here in Oxford, now. Do you want me to go ahead and buy it outright, subject to the deeds being in order, survey carried out, etc? Or would you rather I wait till March?'

'No, you go ahead and buy it, darling. Get on to Susanne right away. We've never had a better lawyer. I'm sure the place is lovely, and you have the best nose I know for property.'

'Okay, darling. The children love the place, too.'

'Even better.'

'Want to speak with them?'

'Love to.'

Chapter 16

The children were so happy to speak with their father again. They didn't really care they were obliged to call him Robert. Robert was a nice name, and in any case they knew it was their dad. Whilst Sally could hardly wait to call him daddy again, young Adam had already begun to appreciate the true reason for the game. He was catching on to the meaning of 'compromise', not solely from a dictionary but from an intelligent discussion with his mother.

Indeed, on the way back to London when Sally had dropped off to sleep with the warmth and movement of the car, Amanda and Adam had picked up the pieces of their conversation about religion and wars, and moved on to the subject of Robert Smythe and their future life with him. This was the stuff of a paperback thriller. And if Adam could hide his true identity, he would have a distinct advantage over many other writers in this genre. To be actually living out a worldwide plot involving big companies, governments and secret agencies was a gift-horse beyond his wildest dreams. To look it in the mouth would be to throw away a golden opportunity for a career as a popular writer. Ah yes, if only he could hold his counsel for ever, those guarded secrets could provide him with a dozen novels. His imagination would do the rest.

The more he thought on these lines, the more Adam realized how lucky he was. He was eager to get started on his book as soon as they had moved into the manor. Besides, he would then be able to have wonderful talks with his father about it. As long as he changed all the names, as encouraged by his mother, and used a nom de plume, everything would be hunky-dory.

They were nearing London, and Sally suddenly sat up in the back of the 4 by 4...

'Have I been asleep, Adam?'

'You have, Sally. Any nice dreams?'

'Oh yes. I dreamt about the manor. You, mummy and daddy were all there and I was playing the harpsichord in The Long Gallery. And then the lady who I think appeared to mummy came over and stood behind me.'

'What happened then?' asked Adam, still somewhat peeved not to be in on the ghost lark.

'I could feel her smiling at me from behind as she guided my hands and fingers. Then I began to play as if by magic. I was so happy.'

'What a lovely dream, Sally.' Amanda made a left turn on to The North Circular. 'And now you're awake, darling, I want to talk to you and Adam about the need for continual secrecy. Even about the manor. Are you with me?'

'I am, mum. But what about Sally?'

'I haven't forgotten, mummy, when you and daddy made us both promise to keep those secrets.'

'Good, darling. But you know, it's for ever. You see, if any of us let slip that Robert Smythe is really Carl Himmler whom I married and who is your father, we'll all be in the soup, and we'll have no peace from the press. Our lives would be sheer hell. So please, please, children, don't ever talk about daddy's change of name to anyone, even to grandpa. At some stage, I might find a way to tell him. But not yet. Okay?'

'Okay, mummy.'

'You have my word, mum.'

Amanda began to relax as she negotiated the roads to the West End. She had already made a call to her lawyer after Robert had spoken to the children. An appointment was made for 4p.rn. today... And now they were making good progress towards Cavendish Square. As the 4 by 4 nosed its way up Wigmore Street, Sally came up with a 'practical' suggestion:

'Mummy, could we eat in San Marino's again this evening while we're this side of the park?'

'Why not, Sally? Adam?'

'Yes, mum. I'd love us to.'

'All right. Would you like to dial the number now? It's in my black book: in the glove box.'

'Okay.' Adam had soon found the book and the number, and dialled the restaurant.

'Certainly, master Adam. We'll reserve the grotto table for you. See you later.'

They left the car in the underground park, and made for the solicitor's office.

'Now, children. Not a word about daddy staying in the house. The lawyer must still think daddy is dead. I am buying the property myself - for our weekend get-aways, got it?'

The children gave their word, and Amanda felt reassured.

'And the same when we go to San Marino's, right, mummy?'

'Right, darling. Good girl. You're getting the idea. All this is still strange to you, I know, but it's all in a good cause.'

'To get daddy back?'

'Yes, dear. Absolutely correct.'

The meeting with Susanne, the lawyer, went smoothly and pleasantly enough, and Adam and Sally said how excited they were about the manor. Amanda almost missed a heart-beat as Sally spoke with such feeling to Susanne...

'I miss daddy lots, Susanne. But I hope mummy marries again soon, and then at least.., at

114

least we'll have a step-father.' Susanne smiled sweetly and cupped Sally's head in her hand. She turned to Amanda with:

'You have a lovely little girl, here, Amanda. And a fine young boy. You must be very proud of them.'

'I am, Susanne. A Godsend, I assure you.'

So, with a phone call to David Reid of Oxford made satisfactorily, Susanne agreed to prepare the contracts for the purchase of the manor. A date for completion would be printed in the documents: 1st March. Susanne would make sure the property was sound and free of debts, and that there would be no hold-up in the proceedings.

With 'hasta la vista' exchanged round the room, Amanda and the children left the law offices of Howard Kennedy and emerged into Cavendish Square. The sun even obliged, sending its warm rays, it seemed, on loan from sunny Spain, c/o Susanne Miranda who had left her native country to become a European high-flier. Ah well, it was the price to pay. And then Amanda was struck with an idea. Maybe it was the sun which did it...

'Look, children. Why don't we make a day of this, and before we go to dinner, pay a visit to Steinways? it's just off Wigmore Street, in

Marylebone Lane. We can leave the car where it is for a while, and walk round. What do you say?'

'Okay, mum.'

'Can we have a tinkle on one of the pianos, mummy?'

'I would hope so, darling. After all, grandpa bought the one we have in the house from the same place. And you ought to practise a little more, Sally.'

'I promise, mummy. But what about Adam?'

'You, too, darling,'

'I know, mum. But what with the worry of all this business, and…'

'Oh Adam. You're getting to sound like an old man. Leave the worrying to me. In any case, your father would be pleased to hear you've been working in his absence.'

'What about my book?'

'You said you'd begin that project in earnest when we're all together in the manor. And then you could, as it were, do your research with Robert. What's to stop you playing the piano in the meantime?'

Adam was stumped. His mother, as usual, had thought of everything, and was looking at him with her endearing, quizzical face.

Chapter 17

Meanwhile, below the water's surface, HMS Astute patrolled the seas of the globe and lurked wherever she willed. Her job was to protect the UK and much of the free world. But who could say if she would retaliate with her deadly missiles on the order of the Prime Minister?

Pampered with excellent food and fine liquor, Commander McGregor and Robert Smythe held regular 'seminars' in the captain's cabin. Soon Robert would be free. Yet doubts had already surfaced in his mind. Surely he was for ever a marked man? If the 'Powers that Be' had spared him his life on the understanding he would change his name, remarry Amanda, and keep out of the armaments business, he could still pose considerable danger to the establishment if he chose to leak information. But then, what they did to Dr. David Kelly they could do to him. It was all down to his tongue. If he controlled it, and submerged himself in harmless, more artistic pursuits, he would be safe. Or would he?

'For Christ's sake, man. Ye canno' carry on worrying for the rest of ye life. Give yeself a break. You owe it to Amanda and the kids.'

'You're right, Malcolm. You're right.' Robert took another sip of his Dalwhinnie whisky, and pondered. 'I think I shall take up a new career.'

The Commander raised his eyebrows as Robert announced: 'Amanda gave me the cue over an intimate dinner in London... Showbusiness.'

Malcolm McGregor's face struggled between an incomplete smirk and an hysterical guffaw. For once in his life, he was at a complete loss for words. Robert stepped in to help him out...

'I can sense,' he said with a wry smile, 'you don't quite picture me in that field. A bit of a change, eh, old man?'

At last Commander McGregor realigned his face and pulled himself together.

'Well, my friend, it's a wee shock, to be honest, unless of course...'

'Yes?' Robert was keen to hear more. He had begun to loosen up. The Dalwhinnie was certainly helping, and in such a delightful manner.

'Unless,' hesitated the Commander, 'well, I'm not sure I should say this, especially to such a fine-looking German gentleman as yeself...'

'Englishman, sir, don't forget... With perhaps a touch of Irish blood tucked in. Go on with your suggestion...'

'Unless ye play Hitler in 'The Producers'. Mel Brooks at his best.'

'Bull's eye, Malcolm. That's exactly what I suggested to Amanda.'

'Another wee dram, Robert?'

'Why not?'

Both men might by now have been in danger of a slight loss of control were it not for their experience as seasoned drinkers, particularly Commander Malcolm McGregor in the whisky department. Only Winston Churchill, in his time, could have outclassed the Commander's capacity for alcohol without its affecting his ability to do his job. And Robert, it seemed, was quickly catching on to the idea. Not that he needed much prompting. There was a short sharp rap on the cabin door, and Commander McGregor was quick to respond.

'Come in.'

The Lieutenant Commander put his head round the door.

'Sorry to disturb you, Commander, but something requires your immediate attention.'

'Thank you, Bill. I'm on my way. Excuse me, Robert. Help yourself to whisky. I'll be back in a jiffy.'

Could this be another Iranian scare? Was HMS Astute about to launch her missiles on foreign soil and start World War Three? Or had it already begun?

Above ground on English soil, Amanda occupied herself with looking after the children, the boutique, and making preparations for Robert's move to Oxfordshire. The owners of the manor had declared themselves happy with the agreed sale price, considering it would be no-nonsense cash, and no 'chain' complications. The Completion date of 1st of March suited them well, and for Amanda there would just be enough time to make the house more than comfortable. Her standards were high, and she had the money with which to indulge her tastes. She was sure Robert would be delighted with the result and could unwind and begin to forget the pressures that for so long had been put upon him. In the course of time, she hoped to join him in the manor and unwind with him. She could hardly wait.

As for the children, time dragged too much for their liking. But then, they were normal, healthy children, longing for the return to the stable family life that had so dramatically been taken from them. Much had happened in that short time to kick them off balance, but their mum had been a tower of strength, and they thanked 'the man in the sky' for his love. At least, this was Sally's line. Besides, she had been privileged to 'touch' the other world and be touched by it. The manor's ghosts were simply charming, as far as she was concerned, and for once, she was one up on her brother Adam. Perhaps, in this respect, he was a late-developer. But time would tell. The landline rang in the London house. It was for mummy.

'Oh, hello, David. What's news?'

'Hi, Amanda. Just to say the owners are happy for you to go ahead and make any alterations to the manor before March 1st, if you so wish.'

'Good Heavens, David. They are trusting. We haven't completed yet.'

'I know. But they don't believe the famous Amanda will go back on her word.'

'Nor will I. That's fantastic. That will help a lot, and please thank them for me.'

'Of course.'

'Keep in touch, David, and I will with you. I'll call you when I'm next in Oxford. You have my lawyer's number, here in London, I trust?'

'Yes, indeed. Speak to you soon, Amanda.'

The television in the drawing-room had been turned up and Amanda found Adam glued to the fearful screen. The Iranian President was screaming violent threats against the West, and the other nations of the world including some peaceful Arab countries were voicing their concern.

'Does this mean world war, mum?'

'I sincerely hope not, Adam.' Amanda's thoughts turned to the submarine where Robert was ensconced with the Commander and crew. She knew its job was to strike out in defence of the realm, if and when necessary. But would the order come from an independent British Prime

Minister, or would it really come from someone in The White House?

She tried to bury these thoughts and concentrate upon Robert's release. But it was difficult. If war were imminent, wouldn't the submarine be required to do its duty? Could the authorities be expected to lose sight of Robert Smythe at such a critical time?

Her mobile buzzed again. It's cheerful little tune seemed less cheerful now, as if events were already taking another nasty turn.

'Hello?'

'Amanda. It's Arthur here. I've been moved to an office of my own in the MI6 building.'

'Moved? It's sounds as though you've been elevated, Arthur. Congratulations.'

'Thanks.., though I'm not exactly unknown to them, you know. But listen, Amanda. Disappointing news, I fear.'

She could guess. Robert would have to stay on the boat until the Iranian crisis blew over.

'That's right, Amanda,' confirmed Arthur Biggs. 'We all hope, of course, the crisis with Iran will be diffused diplomatically. But who can tell? The Iranians are slippery blighters, are they not? Er.., that's strictly off the record, you understand.'

'Of course, Arthur. I presume the sub will stay close at hand to warn off Iran?'

'Well, they have no idea where the boat is. We and the Americans will no doubt warn them strongly to keep their hands off Israel, or they could get the shock of their life.'

'Brinkmanship, eh, Arthur? Like Kennedy and the Cuban crisis?'

'Exactly. But let's hope the situation will ease, and Robert can look forward to March 15th. Keep smiling, Amanda.'

Chapter 18

Keep smiling, he had said. Easy for him, thought Amanda, tucked away in his new London office – a liaison officer between different branches of the law: the establishment, government departments, secret services, The Prime Minister and God knows who else. His knowledge and information must be vast. Despite an apparent glib tongue on occasions over the phone, his secrets would be the envy of even the most successful thriller authors. And to think her own son desired to be among them. With the right agent and publisher, on the other hand, surely his story would give the lad a head start? And what a story. She was living it.

But what about the fate of Robert? Don't panic, she told herself. Don't weaken now. The children need my strength. Yes, she must believe everything would come right in the end. Believe, believe, she told herself. Moreover, the odd prayer or two might not come amiss. Wasn't a crisis just the occasion when people prayed to HIM out there, to someone who must have all the answers?

'What are your thinking, mum?' Young Adam had turned his attention from the rude television to his pensive mother.

'Lots of things, darling, but mostly about daddy and his return to us.'

'Cheer up, mum. As you yourself say, it won't be long now.'

'Except that your father might be a little delayed, owing to the current crisis.'

'Oh no.'

'Officer Biggs has just rung me on my mobile. He has a new office in the MI6 building.'

'Gosh, he must know a few things.'

'Yes, darling. So if you keep your head down, as they say, you might be able to glean quite a number of snippets for your books.'

'I notice you say books, not just book, mum.'

'Well? You believe in yourself, don't you, Adam?'

'Ah mum, you're wonderful. But what did Officer Biggs say?'

'Quite a number of things. But the main reason for his call was the current Iranian situation, and therefore the possibility that Robert would have to remain on the boat until the crisis is over.'

'Oh, here we go again. Disappointment after disappointment.'

'That's life, darling, with perhaps a dash of garlic and black pepper.'

'Is that going to make it better?'

Amanda smiled. She needed cheering up, and her son's banter was a welcome comfort.

Amanda and Adam together decided not to tell Sally about a possible delay in Robert's release. Otherwise, they'd never get any peace. They'd wait for the crisis to be resolved before telling her anything more. They kept their fingers crossed that in a week's time the Iranians would see sense and back off.

They were right. Within the week, through tough negotiation on all sides, the Iranian President climbed down and delivered an equitable and conciliatory speech. The nations of the world had at the last moment formed a consensus of opinion and judgement which the Iranians would do well to recognize. With America, the UK, France, Russia and China lined up against them, where would they go? They knew America had no legitimacy to bomb them, but they also knew that one or other of the Big Powers could and would wipe them off the map from missile strikes if Israel were attacked. Would Iran rather wait for Israel to bomb their installations? The eyes of the world were watching, and the Big Powers were now determined that no Arab country should have the bomb.

'But surely, mum, it's hardly fair Israel should have the bomb, and not Iran?'

'That may seem so, Adam, but the Big Powers don't see it that way. They know that certain Arab nations have proved to be irresponsible hot-heads, or at least their leaders. Can you imagine if

Saddam Hussein had had the bomb? The mayhem he would have unleashed?'

'Yes, I can see that. He fancied himself as Hitler, I think.'

'Could be. And now we have Iran: much more dangerous.'

'Gosh. I didn't know you were so interested in politics?'

'Ah well, my boy, now you know your mum is not just…'

'A pretty face? Golly, this is great stuff. I think I'll have a bash on the Steinway.'

Amanda's eyes lit up. Adam had actually volunteered to bring her beautiful piano alive. But would he do it? He had taken regular piano lessons at school, but was this enough?

He sat on the piano stool and settled himself. To her amazement, he delivered a tender interpretation of Beethoven's Moonlight Sonata - Slow Movement. He even managed the minor 9th span in the right hand, clearly revelling in the poignant clash as ordered by the great composer. So, was her son a genius, a dark horse as yet unrecognized, or just a very bright boy whose light would fade with the cruel passage of time? The spell was rudely broken with the buzz of Amanda's mobile.

'Oh, Arthur. What's news?'

'Just to say, Amanda, that we are hoping to keep to the plan, now Iran has seen sense.'

'Let's hope so, Arthur. We saw the news on the box. Just shows you the Big Powers can do it - when they have the will.'

'Exactly. How have the children taken all this, my dear?'

'Pretty well, in the circumstances. Adam, as you can imagine, is quite pragmatic, and a great comfort to me. Sally misses her daddy terribly: we decided it was best not to say anything about delays and so on.'

'Very wise, Amanda. Let's hope Iran behaves herself, and we can release Robert as scheduled. I'll keep you posted all the way.'

'Thanks, Arthur. We'll all have a celebration dinner when this is over, shall we?'

'Why not? I look forward to the day. ''Bye for now, Amanda.'

''Bye, Arthur.'

The next few weeks were taken up with alterations, decorations and new furnishings for the manor, and the exchange of contracts. 1st of March was fast approaching, and at last Sally had agreed her pining for daddy should be shelved until the day of his release. Then her joy would dissolve all her problems.

Amanda and Adam kept their beady eyes on the box whenever convenient in order to keep abreast of events in The Middle East. The President of Iran, it seemed, had finally decided to enter into a productive relationship with the West. Everyone breathed a sigh of relief, whilst the cynics bit the bullet till the next crisis.

All was looking good, and Amanda's spirits rose by the day. Her lawyer, Susanne Miranda, had agreed to supervise the completion on the house, and have lunch with Amanda and the family at The Trout before returning to London.

'Are we staying in the manor, mummy?'

'Of course, Sally. You want to see your favourite ghost again, don't you?'

'Oh mummy. Don't laugh. She's real to me.'

'I know, dear. I'm not laughing at you. I believe in ghosts, remember? And more.'

'More?'

'Well, I believe we all go to another dimension when we die. Some people would call it Heaven, Sally. But ghosts may well be earthbound, and unable or unwilling to leave the earth plane. Do you follow me?'

'I think so, mummy.'

Chapter 19

The first two weeks of March literally flew by, even for the children, so occupied were they with private tuition - to make up for the gap in the term. Their father's 'funeral' had set them back, but their respective schools were sympathetic, even to the extent of granting them a longer vacation than the other pupils would enjoy. This would enable Amanda and the children to occupy the manor and give it that lived-in feel. Yet ghosts would not be encouraged, if not exactly banned. After only one night at the manor, Amanda put it gently to Sally: 'I'd keep quiet about ghosts, darling, when daddy returns.'

'Okay, mummy.'

'I'm sure he has an open mind about such things, but for the time being at least, I think we should allow him to relax in his own way. Do you agree?'

'Yes. Of course.'

'Good girl.'

'Now, you two. We could rustle up some lunch here, today, or...'

'The Trout.' Quick as a flash, Sally and Adam had suggested it in unison. They both laughed at their own cheek, and Amanda smiled understandingly.

'You and your Trout Inn and San Marino restaurants. You're both more conservative than I thought: conservative with a small 'c', you understand?'

'Yes, mum. Could we?' Adam pleaded with those seductive eyes of his, and Amanda melted.

'My word, you're going to break someone's heart one day, Adam.'

Adam made no plain denial, and appeared to understand very well...

'Plenty of time for that sort of thing, mum.'

His mother smiled anew and continued:

'Okay, let's go, shall we? They're going to think us a bit strange, lunching there again – two days running.'

'Just blame it on us, mum.' Adam was full of ideas, and if they got him his way as a result, so much the better.

Over lunch at The Trout, the three of them laughed and joked about their present predicament, and discussed future plans for their restored life with Mr Robert Smythe. Amanda was just on the point of putting a succulent piece of beef into her mouth when her mobile buzzed.

'Arthur here, Amanda.'

'Good or bad news, Arthur?' She needed certainty now. There had been enough pissing about.

'It's good, Amanda, don't worry. Just to inform you of our plans for releasing him from the boat, and then a safe journey home.'

131

'What do you have in mind?'

'Leave the details to us, Amanda. What we need to know is your new country address so that we can drive him there, after his debriefing. Okay?'

'Well.., Arthur.' She had been loath to divulge the address of the manor for a variety of reasons. To begin with, she felt entitled to one or two secrets herself. God knows, Officer Biggs just had to have a bundle of them, most if not all of which he'd be unwilling to share. On his own admission, she had been misled somewhat on the excuse of avoiding anxiety to her and the children. Why couldn't she meet Robert at an agreed venue, say at a railway station or airport, and then bring him back herself to his new home in the manor?

She had to think quickly, otherwise Arthur's suspicions would be aroused, and he'd find out what he needed to know, anyway, and put a tail on her. Besides, when the time came to announce her engagement to Robert Smythe, the papers would dig and dig, and what would be the point in denial? Dangerous. She should be thankful she had her man back without the world knowing the real truth.

'Okay,' she said at last. 'I wanted it to be my secret, Arthur. But I dare say you'd find out anyway.'

'Indubitably, my dear.'

My word, Officer Biggs had blossomed. He had become posh, since he'd left Paddington

Green. MI6 agents and their associates were certainly expected to be well educated, but could they all match Graham Greene?

Amanda gave Officer Biggs the address of the manor with good grace. He thanked her and offered his assurances...

'Please don't worry, Amanda. Nothing's going to happen to you or Robert or your lovely little family. All of you have played this game magnificently, if I may say so. The rewards are immeasurable: a peaceful, stress-free life with plenty of money - preferable, certainly for Robert, I should say, to a nail-biting existence in the dangerous, murky world of the armaments business.'

'Makes sense to me, Arthur. I know my own father would agree with you.'

'You haven't told him, I hope, about Robert being the very same Carl Himmler?'

'No, I haven't. And I don't intend to, either. But my father is pretty smart, Arthur, and very intuitive.'

'Well, let him raise the subject himself. Don't offer.'

'Believe me, I shan't. It'll make life a lot easier.'

Arthur smiled to himself, and wished Amanda well, passing on his kind regards to the children.

'I'll ring you again a couple of days before 15th. Okay, Amanda?'

'Fine, Arthur, and thanks for your call. I shall be in or around the manor; certainly in the Oxford area.'

'Good. 'Bye for now, my dear.'

''Bye now.'

Amanda switched off her mobile, and got back to her steak. It still tasted good, and the children waited upon their mother to spill the beans about their dad.

Over dessert they talked about the arrangements for Robert's homecoming. How exciting it all was, especially for Sally. Oh, the kisses and hugs she would give her daddy, in spite of the beard. She was not sure whether she'd approve. But if it really was her daddy, it wouldn't matter, would it? He would be home.

Adam, too, was getting excited, though his brain veered on to a different track to Sally's. Already, his mind was tracing the likely manner of his father's extraction from the submarine. If the vessel were obliged to remain on patrol in case Iran reneged on her promises to the world, Robert would probably be pulled off by helicopter. The sub would briefly surface, with the chopper hovering over the turret, and the job could be completed in a few minutes. The helicopter would transport Robert to the airport from whence he'd be flown to the UK in an RAF jet to Lyneham. From there he'd be taken in another helicopter to a safe house for debriefing. A car would then bring him home to his family in Oxfordshire... And what a welcome he'd receive...

'Adam, darling. Where are you? You're miles away.'

'Oh, just imagining Robert's release from the sub. How it'll be done and all that.'

'I expect he'll tell us when he's home. I want to give him a big welcome, and a big dinner - with wonderful food, waiters and music. What d'you think, guys?'

'Lovely, mummy.'

'Better not have the music too loud. We don't want to attract trouble, first night he's home.'

'Good thinking, Adam. So what about piano music? Just you and Sally?'

'Ah, come on, mum. We want him to enjoy himself.'

Chapter 20

15th March… And Amanda hoped Robert Smythe would be 'delivered on the mat' in good shape. Officer Biggs had kept his word to ring Amanda a couple of days before the event, which gave MI6 just enough time to debrief Robert, check his mental health and issue him his new identity papers, passport and so on.

Moreover, the point of the secluded manor was the maintenance of privacy, so essential for the time being. Amanda's natural desire to give her man a glitzy welcome was adeptly tempered, not only by her own self-control but by her bright young son, Adam, who realized the need for tranquillity, if not exactly morbid secrecy. She was not too proud to take his advice on this issue. Yet her blood continued to race with anticipation…

At 6.30 p.m. local time, the car containing Robert, Arthur and an M16 agent drew up outside the security gates that she had agreed to have erected. The password was given, and she excitedly pressed the button to allow the car entrance to the drive. The vehicle swept to a halt on the gravel, and she opened the front door. As Robert climbed the steps to the manor, her arms opened wide to embrace him. Oh, the joy of seeing him again, and looking so well. The beard suited him. He stood there for a few moments to look at her. She looked at him, his fine hair beginning to grey in the right places; the smile his, and his alone.

'Oh my darling man. Welcome home.'

'Amanda.'

The children crowded round their passionate parents with barely controlled tears of joy. Robert lifted them both off their feet, and smothered them with kisses and cuddles. Amanda's tears flowed on, and she reached for her handkerchief which was fast becoming hopelessly inadequate for the task. But what a task. They were all so happy.

Then Robert introduced the MI6 agent, Barry Ross, and of course, reintroduced Arthur Biggs who had, in Amanda's book, finally turned up trumps. How could she ever have doubted him?

They relaxed at last, and entered the house to begin a very special celebration.

'Oh daddy, I like your beard.'

'Do you, Sally? Not too prickly for you?'

'No. Just right.'

The men smiled, and knew it would be difficult for Sally to desist from calling him daddy. But this, after all, was a very special night, and everyone partaking of dinner was privy to the plot.

Adam, by contrast, chose to play the actor, once his father had released him from his embrace. 'Robert, you look fantastic. Good to see you again.'

'And you, Adam. You've grown swiftly to become the man of the house, I hear. I may have to fight you to regain my position.'

'I don't think so,' flashed Adam with a manly smile, while the tears of joy still flowed in his eyes.

'Now, folks.' Amanda struggled to gain control of the evening. 'Barry, Arthur, would you like to give me your coats? I'll put them in here.' She hung them together with Robert's in the new cloakroom she had had constructed.

'I'll show you all round the house later. But first I think we need a drink.'

She ushered the men and the children into a beautiful reception room, and there, standing behind a large table, were two smart MI6 waiters, eager to serve. Amanda had readily agreed with Arthur for security reasons.

'By golly, Amanda, you don't spare the horses,' joked Robert.

'Why should I, darling? The fatted calf will come later.'

He laughed, and Arthur and Barry looked on with amusement and satisfaction.

'Would you care to look after our guests for a moment, Robert, while I have a word with the chef?'

'Good idea, Amanda. Have you got him from MI6, too?'

'Of course, darling. Best not disturb Luigi's and Dembrey's respective equilibriums. They're both in London.'

Arthur Biggs grinned approvingly. Amanda could be trusted to keep matters on a tight rein until her engagement and ultimate marriage to Robert Smythe. The tongues could wag as much as they liked, then.

She had quickly returned, and announced to the party that dinner would be served in the dining-room in fifteen minutes. It would be a simple meal of fresh asparagus soup, Scotch smoked salmon and rare rib beef, followed by rich sherry trifle with cream for dessert. Coffee and liqueurs, naturally, would follow...

The doors to the dining-room were opened, and the party entered into the splendour of a tapestry-lined room, the large candle-lit table laden with silver cutlery, bone china plates and fine cut-glass goblets. Bottles of fine French wine lined one of the sideboards close to the table, and any appreciative eye could sense the evening would hardly be that dry.

The two happy waiters bustled round the room, putting in place large tureens, filled with mashed and roasted potatoes, cauliflowers and peas. They smiled and signalled Amanda that they were ready.

'Okay, you happy people. If you'd care to take your places, we can begin.'

'Thank you, Amanda.'

'Oh darling. This is wonderful.' Robert held Amanda close and they kissed warmly. She could already feel him getting hard, but this was not the time or the place for it. He'd have to be patient. He smiled a knowing smile. 'All right, I will be sensible,' he whispered. She said nothing, but he knew she felt the same, and wanted him badly. It would not be such a long wait. In the meantime, they could smell the gorgeous food, and the children were anxious to be with him.

'Could I sit next to d..? I'll try to call him Robert as we get going, mummy. But it might be difficult.'

'I'm sure you can do it, Sally.'

Amanda smiled through those joyful tears which started to well again in her eyes. What fabulous kids I have, she thought. What would I have done without them?

'Mum, may I sit the other side of Robert, and perhaps I could talk to Mr Ross across the table?' Adam could hardly wait to quiz the secret service man.

'Of course you may sit next to Robert. But be careful what you say to Mr Ross, darling. You know he's a real MI6 agent?'

'Of course. That's why I want to talk to him.'

'Well, go easy, dear. Listen carefully to what he has to say, too. You do tend to go hell for leather.'

'All right, mum. I'll listen. All good training, this.' Adam bristled with pleasure and excitement.

He was on a mental high. Perhaps if he could one day join MI6, he might turn out to be another Graham Greene. What more could he ask?

Robert smiled and relaxed anew, soaking up the atmosphere of this wonderful house where he'd rejoined his loving family. A gentle wave of contentment began to wash over him, as if he'd entered The Kingdom of Heaven for the first time, as if all his work, arguments, fights, love and sex, care for his wife and children, achievements and disappointments, money made and spent, sins committed, sins of omission - everything had converged to this point, this precious moment. If he died right now, he would have had a full life. He felt as though God were watching, not in admonishment or anger, not in judgement, but love. Real love. His family - Amanda, Sally and Adam - this magic moment in this magic manor: could he ever conjure it all again?

As they settled in their seats and the candles flickered over the elegant table, they raised their glasses to one another and to a unique family reunion, strangely watched over by two ever increasingly mellow outsiders, Arthur Biggs and Barry Ross. If Scotland Yard and MI6 could see them now. But then, cynical, hard men of the world were human, too. Policemen and secret agents drank alcohol like other people; and doesn't MI6 arrange murder only when necessary? Whose body was it they found on the bench in Hyde Park?

Adam's brain was working at full speed. He desperately wanted to open up a conversation with Mr Ross, but he wisely decided to wait until the man had 'had a few', and then hit him with a succinct question. Barry Ross engaged in small talk across the table, and Adam bided his time. Much to his surprise, he hadn't long to wait.

'So, what do you want to do when you leave school, young man?' Barry's clear blue eyes searched Adam's face for any weakness or hesitation. But Adam was ready for him.

'I want to go to Oxford, and then train for the secret services.'

'Oh? And why do you imagine this will be an exciting life, unless you decide to become a spy?'

'I never want to be a spy, Mr Ross. But I'd like to catch one.'

'Very difficult, Adam, until it's too late. We know this to our cost.'

'But the Cold War is over, isn't it?' Adam would not give up.

'The world, I fear, is no less dangerous a place for that.'

'So we still need spies, then?'

'Of course.'

This conversation was already beginning to worry Amanda, but the men were highly amused and very impressed by young Adam. His father more than proud. He knew he would soon be having long discussions with his son on many issues, but there was plenty of time. This one between Barry Ross and Adam was just warming up.

'However,' continued the secret agent, 'the areas of danger have moved, somewhat, to put it mildly. Militant Islam is a big problem for the West, and the tools of war, as you must know, are no longer a matter of swords and arrows. What is your opinion, for instance, of Abu Hamza, the man we warned the government about for too many years?'

God, that was a mouthful from agent Ross. Adam had still not planted his succinct question. Barry Ross, it seemed, had taken the initiative, and was delving deep into young Adam's mind. But the lad was well up to the task:

'Abu Hamza, in my opinion, Mr Ross, should have been chucked out of this country long ago. Anyone with a brain could see he was up to no good.'

'Exactly, Adam. Unfortunately, this country is still stuck in the mire of political correctness. There comes a point when one must stand up and uphold the values of one's own country. Agreed?'

'Agreed. And what's more, the lead should come from the government. If they are too frightened to do it, they shouldn't be in government.'

'Well said, sir.' Barry Ross had begun to appreciate young Adam's intelligence and way with words, but wished to press him further. 'But what exactly should they do?'

'Simple. The Prime Minister should appear on television and lay it down calmly and directly. "When in Rome, you do as the Romans do. If you don't like the British way of life, leave. We couldn't do what we like in your country. So it's a simple choice."' Adam stopped short, surprised by his own torrent of words. When the applause for his 'speech' had died down, Barry Ross leant across the table, closer to Adam, to make his quiet remark: 'He wouldn't have the guts.'

Adam agreed with Mr Ross, and reached for his glass. He would be allowed a little wine tonight, on this very special occasion. Robert smiled on him and gave him a big hug. No father could have been prouder. And now it was Sally's turn to be heard, and much to the surprise and delight of the gathering, she spoke in the hope that Robert would soon marry mummy. She said it in such a way as though this were the first meeting between the two...

'I think Robert fancies mummy, don't you, Mr Ross?'

'I did catch the odd glance of affection, yes, Sally. And after all, he hasn't exactly been slow in embracing and kissing your mother. I think we ought to marry them off before anything else happens, don't you?' Barry Ross smiled tenderly towards Sally. It was the first time she'd seen him let go in such a human way. Everyone laughed and the waiters rallied to refill the glasses, so engrossed had the company been in the conversation between Adam and Barry. But now it was time for the soup, and comparative quiet descended as they spooned the delicious, creamy starter. Succulent salmon and bloody beef would follow, and then no doubt the conversation would heat up again. It would certainly be a night to remember.

Chapter 21

The eating and drinking continued unabated while laughter and conversation permeated the elegant room. It was not long before Amanda considered that unless Arthur and Barry wished to drive back to London through the night in a perilous condition, they had better stay until morning.

'We've left it open with our families, Amanda,' said Arthur wistfully, looking up at the lady of the manor from his comfortable chair - with hopes of her offering to put them up in real four-poster beds. 'Barry and I have prepared our wives for our night out on the tiles.' They all laughed.

'Well, that's settled then,' responded Amanda contentedly. 'You'll both be very comfortable, I can assure you.'

'Extremely kind, Amanda, thanks. I trust Barry and I are not expected to sleep together?'

'Of course not, Arthur. A bedroom each.' Amanda smiled, and Arthur relaxed again.

The desserts were served and then on came the coffees, brandies and liqueurs. Arthur lit up a magnificent Havana as Barry looked on, happy with his coffee and brandy.

'I must say, Amanda, you have done us proud. Thank you.' The secret agent no longer looked so secretive. He seemed like a harmless, grateful lost soul who had been brought in from the cold to be fed and watered. He was anything but harmless: a priceless friend but a lethal enemy.

'It's a pleasure, Barry.' She turned to the rest of the party. 'Shall we all take our drinks into the lounge and have a little music?'

'What have you in mind, darling?'

'You'll see, Robert. I think you'll approve.'

Adam could sense his mother was about to ask him to play his Beethoven party piece from the Moonlight Sonata - that famous piece of serious music for the sensitive soul. Sally guessed she'd be asked to play a little magical Mozart. She would be ready. Into the drawing-room they trooped, while the waiters cleared the dining-table.

And what a drawing-room. Newly decorated with great taste, it nevertheless retained its Elizabethan structure, features and feel whilst providing 'modern' comfort in the manner of magnificent leather sofas and armchairs, and Persian carpets which had never seen better days. The Steinway 'B' Grand stood in the corner on a polished oak floor. The lid of the piano was fully raised, and the instrument had never looked so wonderfully inviting. Robert glanced at Amanda with a tender smile. They said nothing but both savoured the thought: the Steinway had been their wedding present from David Davidson, and Amanda had recently had it moved from Brompton Square to the manor, here in Oxfordshire.

'Sally darling. Would you like to play Robert your Mozart? I know he'd love to hear you.'

'Would you, Robert?'

'Of course, Sally. Please go ahead. We all want to hear you.'

'It's a bit difficult for me, but I'll do my best.'

Indeed, the First Movement of Mozart's Piano Sonata in A minor, Kockel no. 310, is a bit difficult, unless you happen to be Mozart. But Sally was brave, and charged in with gusto. Much to her delight, her fingers flowed as never before. The passion and strength was there, too. Could this be her favourite ghost again? Or a new one? Her mother had advised her to steer clear of the subject until Robert had settled himself in his new home. But sure enough, Sally performed like a professional. The room exploded with rapturous applause, and Sally was covered with heart-felt kisses from all sides. She made a mental note to thank her ghost formally, tonight in bed.

Then it was Adam's turn. He swung on to the piano stool with eager delight, but soon put on his 'serious' face. Could this be Dudley Moore's ghost at work? He warned his audience he would desist from mucking about, and began... This lad could play.

When he'd finished, the room remained silent. He turned to glimpse tears of love in the eyes of his mother and father, and a tender, sisterly smile on Sally's face. Arthur and Barry too had been stunned into silence. Then they all applauded, and came over to hug him, this young boy who had grown into early maturity and had affected them so, touching a nerve, a spiritual chord within them. No one in the room had been left out, and this night would for ever be imprinted upon their souls. Arthur Biggs, who had seen more life and death than he'd care to recall, had succumbed to the charm of the music. And even Barry Ross with his sharp brain and analytical leanings had been affected to the good. How could this family possibly pose a serious threat to The Establishment? As soon as Robert had married Amanda and settled down, the 'manacles' would no longer be needed, and Barry Ross could move on to a new case. There would never be a shortage of work in his department. And he loved it. As long as it never became boring routine 'policing', Barry would be happy. MI6 had long been his métier. Wouldn't it be ironic if this boy Adam were one day to be recruited into the service and overtake him? These things happened.

'But you're not drinking, Barry. Allow me to refresh you.' Robert raised himself from his luxurious armchair, and, taking hold of Barry's glass, walked across to the sideboard on which an array of spirits and liqueurs had thoughtfully been placed.

'Thank you, Robert. Yes, I'd love another cognac, if you have one.'

'Of course.' Robert poured another generous measure into Barry's glass and took it across to him. 'Arthur?'

'I'd appreciate a wee dram of Dalwhinnie which I see you have hiding away on the sideboard.'

Robert laughed. 'Nothing is hiding away tonight, Arthur. Amanda must have bought it for me. I let it slip it was fast becoming my favourite tipple on the boat.'

'Ah, Commander McGregor. A good scout, and what a character.'

'Yes, a fine man. I had many interesting conversations with him. The whisky was a perfect complement.' Robert had poured a healthy measure into Arthur's glass.

'I'll join you in one of these.'

He poured another for himself, and carried the glasses over to where Arthur was sitting. 'And for you, my darling?' He turned to Amanda who had been busy with the children.

'Just a small Amaretto, thanks, Robert.'

'Coming up, my love.'

'The children are getting a little tired, I think.'

'Not I. I'm not tired.' Adam wanted to prove his stamina and show off his grammar at the same time. Everyone laughed, but mum was firm.

'Maybe not, dear, but I want you two in bed. You'll have another chance to speak with Mr Ross tomorrow, Adam, before he returns to London. Breakfast at 8 sharp. Okay?'

'Okay, mum. I'm going, and thank you for a lovely evening.'

'My pleasure, darling, and thank you for playing... Sally? You too, darling. I'm proud of you both.' Hugs and kisses followed, and then Robert joined in to give both his children a loving hug and kiss.

'Goodnight, Officer Biggs. Goodnight, Mr Ross.'

'Goodnight, Adam.., Sally. See you both in the morning.'

When Amanda returned, having settled the children and seeing the waiters and chef safely and contentedly off the premises, she relaxed on a comfortable sofa next to Robert, and abandoned herself to the atmosphere she had done so much to create and maintain.

'I'd like to propose a toast, if I may,' began Arthur Biggs. 'To the reunion of Amanda and her man.'

Smiles lit up their faces as each wondered who'd be the first to mention Carl Himmler. Or was he dead for ever?

'Now, folks,' interjected Robert graciously but firmly before they raised their glasses. 'I prefer to be called Robert from now on. The name is changed for ever, and I'm very comfortable with it.' He grinned at Amanda who nodded her approval.

'So I propose the toast,' continued Arthur Biggs unfazed 'to the reunion of Amanda and Robert.'

'Amanda and Robert.' They raised their glasses and drank. Yet Arthur had more to say. 'But now, I think Barry here would like to outline a few more facts concerning the case of the late Carl Himmler (Wry smiles greeted the name. But they held their tongues and allowed Arthur to continue). I trust it will settle your minds and convince you that this extraordinary plot was carried out, more for the purpose of protecting Robert than a vain attempt to interfere with the course of legitimate business.'

'Do you really want to hear this, darling?'

'Yes, I do, Robert. Thank you for your concern, but now Barry has taken the trouble to come here himself, we might as well benefit from his knowledge of the affair, and put those niggling doubts to rest.'

'Very wise, Amanda.' Arthur Biggs remained impressed with the lady's inquiring mind.

Very well. Over to you, Barry.' Robert relaxed.

'Thank you, Robert. Now, from the very beginning, we have suspected an infiltration of your company from the Middle East 'mafia', call it what you will. We know it's a very serious group of ruthless businessmen. While the world is distracted by suicide bombings, these men seek out their chances to loosen the Western grip on the armaments business. Get my drift?'

'Go on.'

'Well, for some time, we've been monitoring two of your directors in particular who wished to deal with certain Middle East countries without your knowledge. I'll give you the names in a moment. They hoped to take advantage of your absence on your regular trips out of the country to clinch the deals: massive backhanders which would easily cover and be hidden by seemingly bona fide contracts. It's not hard to imagine what could have resulted if these men had had their way.'

Robert gasped, but allowed Barry to continue without interruption. 'Our inside man (he will remain nameless) was the one to cook up the plan of your 'murder' in order to put the frightener on these directors. The plan worked and flushed out both these characters. You know them, of course: Frederick Jurgens, known as Freddie, and Boris Richards, the two men in whose presence, I understand, you chaired a few unpleasant meetings, to put it mildly.'

'God Almighty.' Robert took a bigger sip of his whisky. 'To think I'd had my doubts about their agenda for some time, but couldn't be absolutely sure.' The thought of nuclear bombs in manic Middle Eastern hands by the back door of his own company gripped him with horror.

'I'm afraid,' resumed Barry Ross, 'we used you as the guinea-pig in this experiment, but we by no means finished you off, as I can see.'

'Oh, thank you,' joked Robert.

'You are alive and well - with plenty of money, a beautiful woman and kids, a lovely house here and in London. And (he paused), if you would like your job back as Chairman of the Board, it's yours for the taking.' Barry Ross smiled and waited for the response, but already knew the answer...

'Thank you, but no. I've had enough of that nonsense, Barry. You carry on with your games in MI6. I know Adam would like to join you, but for me...' He turned to Amanda. 'This woman will do me for the rest of my life. We will start again, give Adam and Sally our love and support, and this (he put two fingers up in the air)... to the world.'

He kissed Amanda; and Barry and Arthur looked on, grinning with approval.

Chapter 22

It was lights out at the manor, all except the subtle, sensual lamps of Amanda's bedroom. She wanted to see him in all his glory. He badly needed her, and could hardly wait.

They undressed each other - fondling, kissing, stroking, sucking along the way. Then lustfully Robert slapped her body and 'pushed' her into bed. She did not resist, for she knew he'd been starved of sex for too long, unless...

'Robert, for God's sake. What have you been doing on that bloody boat?'

'Not what you imagine, Amanda. It's never been my scene, even in an emergency.'

She chuckled. So did he, their concentration momentarily broken. But they quickly recovered and settled down to wondrous love-making. On and on it went, the perfect match of male and female, yin and yang and fine shades of both. A combined effort of supreme pleasure, soon to reach its peak...

Then they lay back and talked softly, taking stock of their lives and hopes for the future: plans for their engagement and remarriage. But Robert was on her again, and this time she was going to give him the works. Their moaning and groaning rose to a crescendo, but what the hell? Their bedroom was isolated from the others. Someone had thought things through, and considered privacy to be of prime importance.

And what space. The house had been worked on through the centuries: some alterations for the better, some to the detriment of its cohesion. Styles and tastes would for ever differ between people, but the previous owners of the house had, to Amanda's mind, done a pretty good job in its care and maintenance. David Reid, the estate agent, had surprisingly over-exaggerated the need for restoration. From a purist point of view, it was far from perfect. But Amanda possessed an accommodating mind. Purists could live in a museum if they wished: she would live in a comfortable, elegant home.

Soon it was morning. Toiletries and showers prevailed, and after her own ablutions Amanda scooted down into the spacious kitchen. She would prepare cereals, and cook bacon and eggs for everyone.

Just before 8 a.m. Adam and Sally appeared, looking a shade bleary-eyed but very, very happy.

'Lovely party last night, mummy.'

'Yes, it was,' concurred Adam.

'It was fun, wasn't it, my darlings. Now, tea or coffee?'

'Tea for me, mummy.'

'And for me.'

A grandfather clock chimed the hour in the hallway, and footsteps could be heard, clonking down the stairs like a scaled-down rugby team. It was the three men, who seemed wide awake and ready for action. But then, their lives had been that way.

'Good morning, darling. Haven't I seen you somewhere before?'

'Robert, dear.' She smiled at him with love fulfilled.

''Morning, Amanda.'

'Amanda, can we help?'

'No, gentlemen. Just sit down, would you? Cereals and milk here. Tea and coffee coming up. Bacon and eggs sizzling in the pan. No one has gout, I trust?'

'Not yet, darling. But you never know.'

Adam and Sally laughed and kissed their father. He could always come up with a cheery quip or response. If he'd changed his name to Tom Cruise, they'd still recognize him as their dad... on stilts.

'By the way, mum, who does Robert remind you of?'

'Tom Cruise, mummy?' Sally couldn't wait.

'Yes, he does, now you mention it. I'll be able to take him anywhere, won't I? The only trouble is, I'll have my hands full, keeping all the other women at bay.'

"Tom Cruise" smiled broadly. He was enjoying this.

They sat round the large oak table to partake in a typical English breakfast, with toast and Oxford marmalade to finish. Copious cups of tea would be consumed, for no one had requested coffee. They would reserve that for elevenses. By then, Barry and Arthur would both be back in London, hard at work on new, pressing cases.

Even before they'd finished breakfast, Adam was itching to ask Barry questions about his work. But Amanda's face said it all: leave him to finish in peace. Then, perhaps one succinct question that he might be willing to take on...

'Sally, dear. Would you like to practise the piano, if you've finished your breakfast?'

'All right, mummy. Good idea.' Sally skipped off to the drawing-room to play some more Mozart.

Adam had read his mother's mind. What's more, as for his question, he would not have to make the running. Having downed his last piece of toast and sipped his tea, Barry Ross looked up from the table to Adam with a quizzical expression.

'I sense you wish to ask me something, Adam. Something important to you?'

'Yes. Was it absolutely necessary to go through the farce of Carl Himmler's funeral, and a new identity as Robert Smythe?' Amanda and Robert froze whilst Adam looked Barry straight in the eye without a flicker. It was not so much a cold stare as a firm, serious look of determined enquiry. The secret agent was very impressed.

'Yes, it was, I'm afraid, Adam. Your father will no doubt explain the details in his own time. Suffice to say, MI5 and MI6 are not as terrible as they sound. It's true MI6 does arrange eliminations, whether by 'accident' or otherwise, when there's no better way of dealing with a serious, urgent problem. (Adam's mind flashed to the suspicious death of Princess Diana) Our loyalty, you see, is to the Head of State and the government. From time to time, this entails unavoidably sordid activities when The Establishment faces a threat to its stability and welfare. Are you still interested in that job with MI6, or have I put you off the idea?' Agent Ross kept smiling.

'I'm fascinated, Mr Ross.'

'Well, Adam. I'll keep in touch with your delightful family through Arthur, here. He is far more accessible to you. My work, as I have indicated, does tend to make one invisible. Do you get my meaning?'

'Yes sir, I do.'

'And you may call me Barry. Don't be afraid.'

When they'd all said their goodbyes, Amanda pressed the button to open the security gates. She had the distinct feeling she'd be seeing more of Arthur Biggs in the future, but never again Barry Ross. She couldn't put a finger on the reason for this strong feeling. It was just that it was there. She brushed the idea aside, and made sure the gates were closed when their vehicle had gone.

Then she turned to matters of the family.

'Robert, dear. I didn't get round to showing them over the house. But would you care for a conducted tour?'

'Why not? Thank you, darling.'

'Sally is practising the piano.'

'I was, mummy.' Sally had returned to join in the fun with her daddy.

'Well, at last we're all back together as a family – with no outsiders present,' sighed Amanda contentedly.

'Isn't it wonderful?' Robert began to let out his feelings of joy as he jostled playfully with Adam and then with Sally.

'I'll tell you what,' suggested Amanda happily. 'After the tour of the house, we'll talk about our plans and then have lunch somewhere nice, shall we?'

'Oh yes, mummy. The Trout?' And, of course, Adam agreed with his sister.

'You and your Trout.' So predictable, but Amanda didn't mind. She liked the old inn, and she was sure Robert would approve, too. It was not yet Easter Weekend, so it shouldn't be too crowded. 'Okay,' she continued. 'The Trout Inn it is.'

'Whoopee,' cried the children.

As they toured the house together, Robert made pertinent comments on the many fine features of the building. The Georgian style was still his favourite period of English architecture, yet he could appreciate the charm of an Elizabethan manor. Besides, Amanda had made sure the whole place would be as comfortable as possible. She'd done a fine job.

They had reached The Long Gallery, and Robert suddenly stood stock-still, gazing in wonder at... 'Is this place haunted, Sally?' It was Sally's chance to spill the beans. Amanda smiled on her. 'Ah, but daddy, they are lovely ghosts. Mine is a beautiful lady who plays the harpsichord just here.' Sally pointed out the spot and said: 'And what's more, she helped me last night, when I played my Mozart on the Steinway.' Sally turned again to face her daddy who could see she was deadly serious, and so happy about it. Why then should he feel fear?

'Well, Sally, I shall have to wait for my ghost to come along, won't I? Hope I'm not going to see myself.' Amanda tried to laugh, but couldn't. Robert's remark gave her an uncomfortable feeling, but Sally saved the day: 'Ah, but that would be impossible, daddy, because you didn't die.'

Chapter 23

Amanda phoned The Trout Inn and booked a table for four. 1.30, the manager said, would be fine. That done, she could concentrate on other matters.

Over elevenses, they began to discuss their future life together as the Smythe family. But they would have to set it up properly. It was important that they should not take unnecessary risks. The Trout Inn could hardly be compared with a gossipy London pub, full of journalists and other loose tongues. But there was always the odd bright student or nosy professor hanging about who might fancy his or her chances with a leaked story. So it was better to talk it through now - within the solid walls of this secluded old house.

'Robert, would you care to kick off, as they say?'

'Okay, Amanda. Are we all listening?'

'Yes, daddy...'

'Right. First item is the run-up to the official engagement of the famous fashion designer Amanda to a Mr Robert Smythe.' Smiles round the table accompanied this rather formal statement as Robert continued. 'I suggest, Amanda, we 'happen to meet' in Claridges, one lunchtime. Separate tables, etc. I spot you and send a note via the waiter over to your table, inviting you to join me.'

'Wow. How romantic.'

'All right, Adam.' Amanda blushed.

'You do join me, walking to my table with grace and style. We eat and drink together. The papers catch us as we leave the restaurant, smiling at each other.'

I can see the headlines, now,' interposed young Adam, excited as ever:

THE FAMOUS FASHION DESIGNER,
AMANDA, ANNOUNCES HER ENGAGEMENT TO
MR ROBERT SMYTHE

'Hang on, Adam,' urged Amanda. 'It's just the first meeting, got it?'

'Okay, mum, I'll hang on.'

'The second time the media catch us in Claridges,' resumed Robert, unfazed by Adam's enthusiastic interruption, 'we announce our engagement.'

'Isn't this all a bit complicated?' enquired Sally innocently.

'It is a bit. But you see, Sally, mummy and I want it all to look very natural to the silly world we live in. If we do it this way, we hope no one will suspect I am the same Carl Himmler whose funeral you attended. I know you can act, Sally. And when mummy and I are married, we can stop pretending. After all, you did your bit beautifully last night.'

'When I played the piano?'

'Not only that, but when you spoke to Mr Ross about Robert fancying mummy. Remember? And you remember what he said?'

'Oh yes. Okay, daddy. Anything, anything for you.' She gave her father a big kiss on his cheek.

'I love you, too, Sally. Now, second item to discuss is the announcement of the wedding day. Shall we fix it now, Amanda?'

'Oh yes, mummy. Go on.'

'Steady, Sally darling, let's think. What date do you have in mind, Robert?'

'Let's look at a diary.'

'Here, dad, look through this big one mum bought for the house.' Adam handed his father the large house diary from the kitchen shelf.

'Thanks, Adam... Ah yes.' Robert glanced in the book, turning the pages to the end of summer. He stopped, and turned back to June. 'How about flaming June, Amanda?'

'If you like, Robert.'

'Can we make it June 18th? It's my birthday.' Adam's eyes shone bright with ideas.

'So it is, Adam. But surely you don't want us to overshadow your birthday, darling?'

'Why not, mum? It'll be the best birthday present you and dad could give me.'

'Oh, my darling boy.' Amanda leant across the table to hug her son.

'Thanks, Adam. That's a lovely sentiment. Love you, son.' Robert dabbed a tear with his handkerchief. He could be very emotional at times, and felt glad his family shared his feelings.

'Okay then,' he continued, trying to recover his grip on matters, 'that's two items dealt with.'

'In the meantime, darling, we should decide about living arrangements.'

'Oh yes, Amanda. Are you happy about weekends together as a family, here?'

'Fine by me.'

Amanda explained to the children the wisdom of Robert's stay in the manor until the wedding. The occasional trip to London for 'public outings', as it were, would look good and provide just enough publicity to whet the appetite of the media. After the wedding, Robert could come and live in Brompton Square again. Everything above board, so to speak. The Himmlers and soon to become the Smythes were very old-fashioned. And what was wrong with that?

'Now, Sally, how about playing me that Mozart piece I just heard, drifting from the drawing-room? And then, showing me your latest dress designs?'

'I'd love to, mummy.'

'We'll leave daddy to have a chat with Adam before we make tracks for The Trout. All right?'

'Good idea.' Sally and her mother left the two guys to have a manly chat on their own. It would be good for both of them. Adam, for his part, needed to know more about his father, despite the trips abroad he'd been privileged to take in his company. Their love for each other as father and son also needed to be re-established, and what better time to express it than now?

There was so much Adam wanted to discuss with his father, and so much Robert desired to share with his son. He would take it step by step. Intelligent as the boy undoubtedly was, it might be difficult to explain to him the reason for secrecy in certain areas of life's problems and tests. Adam had shown considerable skill in acting his part while Robert was away, and his probe into the affairs of the secret services had impressed agent Ross. But now had come the time for Robert to lay some more cards of his own on the table. Step by step.

The conversation began with the change of name, not that Adam disapproved of it. In fact, he had liked it from the beginning, and had said so. This encouraged his father who took up the theme with boldness.

'To be honest, Adam, I prefer the name Smythe to Himmler for obvious reasons. Himmler has a terrifying ring to it, on a par I'd say, with Hitler. We know that instructions for the killing of the Jews in the Second World War came from the top - in other words, from Adolf Hitler himself. But it was Himmler who set up and supervised the death camps, and his name will for ever be associated with them. As far as I know, I am not related to that odious creature, but I can't be sure. Himmler, after all, is as common a name in Germany as

166

Smith in this country. Ironically, I have the British Prime Minister and MI6 to thank for my demise as Carl Himmler and my resurrection, if I may put it that way, as Robert Smythe. Do you follow me?'

'Yes, father. I'm already used to your new name. As for the Nazi period, though, I find it hard to imagine what people really felt at the time. The Germans I've met seem a pretty cool lot, to me, but then...' Adam had begun to run out of steam. He knew his own father, this Robert sitting with him, was indeed German. And he was such a nice man.

'Anyway,' said Robert with a smile, 'now is now. Germans have learned to live and work with all nationalities and take their place alongside the rest of the civilized world. It's almost as if the Nazi period had never been.

Now I come to ·the nitty-gritty of the Carl Himmler affair. As Barry Ross indicated, I shall explain it to you in my own way. Well, Adam, I'm not one to pussyfoot around or dodge the issue. You are an intelligent boy and my son whom I love. I shall explain it to you now. Ready?'

'Yes, father.' Adam was all ears. He sat next to Robert, with his coffee near to hand and a few biscuits Amanda left on the table on the understanding he'd not eat too many and spoil his lunch at The Trout which was to follow.

His father explained the idea of the plot as outlined by agent Ross. Adam listened carefully, and his imagination ran wild... God, my book is going to be a blockbuster... When his father had finished, he thanked him for telling him the truth and kissed him. They hugged each other for a while and then Adam brightened up again.

'About my book, dad.'

'Yes, Adam, your mother tells me that far from dropping the idea, you are keener than ever. Of course you have my blessing. Presumably you will change all the names?'

'Naturally'

'Good boy. But what about your own? Even when you change to Smythe, won't people realize your story is about us? Would we get any peace?'

'Don't worry, dad. I shall talk to my agent about that, and seek his advice.'

Robert smiled. His son would never do things by halves. He'd find himself that bloody agent, by hook or by crook.

Chapter 24

Before she had time to brood, Amanda's 'Claridges date' with Robert was upon her.

He had arrived early as planned, and sat at his table in direct line of her agreed entrance. Her table had been booked in the name of Amanda. She was a household name, and respected in all circles of society. But she was only human, with all the human weaknesses intertwined with her tested and inner strengths. Would her nervousness show when she arrived to take her seat? Would he even be there, or if he was, would he suddenly take it into his head to walk over to her as bold as brass, and spoil it all?

She was determined to play-act to the end. After all, she had survived the 'funeral', the burial, and the reunion with the Himmler family. She'd survived his absence, and necessarily sparse, truncated calls, calls and meetings with Arthur Biggs, the waiting, the children's concerns, everything. How could this funny little lunch-date compare with all that?

The waiter had brought her an aperitif and the menu card. She casually glanced through the a la carte, and looked up to where he was sitting. He smiled and lifted his glass in quiet salute. She returned the smile but went no further. She could tell he appreciated her coolness.

She saw another waiter walk over to him, and a note passing hands. The waiter was coming her way.

'Excuse me, Miss Amanda. The gentleman asked me to give you this note. He's sitting over there.'

'Oh, thank you so much.'

The waiter left her to read the note. She steadied her hands…

Please join me at my table

for lunch now.

Regards, Robert Smythe

She looked up from the note, and faced him with a smile and gracious nod of acceptance.

Slowly she rose from her seat, and walked elegantly across to the attractive, bearded man with the charming smile.

'Thank you, kind sir. I'd love to join you.'

'Very good. Have a seat.' He pulled up a chair where they could talk unmolested and out of earshot. Occasionally they touched hands, but only very lightly. Their act was exemplary.

The dining-room began to fill as they ordered lunch. She chose foie gras and roasted cannon of lamb to follow whilst he decided on soup of the day and a blue fillet of beef. An '82 Claret was on its way.

'So,' he began, 'we meet here, of all places. How are you?'

170

'Fine, Mr Smythe. Thank you for your charming note.'

'Not at all. You looked to me an interesting lady, full of life and character and just a little lonely. So I thought, why not ask her over? Hope you don't mind?' He flicked a subtle lift to his eyebrows, and stretched his lips into the smile she knew so well.

'Mind? Why should I mind? I don't usually do this sort of thing, you know, but I thought, well, why not? He seems like a nice man - intelligent, handsome and kind eyes. I always notice the eyes.'

'So do I. Yours are very warm and inviting. Shall I pour?'

'Please do.'

They sipped their claret and began to relax a little and take their time.

The food proved delicious, as expected, and they made a decision to come here again, without fuss.

But just as they began talking quietly about this, they spotted a few cameras at work, snapping away at some theatre characters on the next table. The cameras seemed to come from nowhere, but then a well-known actor spied Amanda, sitting there with Robert.

'Why, it's Amanda herself, I believe. Why don't you go and snap her, my friend, and her new boyfriend?'

The cameraman from The Daily Mail obliged, and came across to Robert's table... Snap, snap, before he could say no. But he wouldn't say no, would he?

'All right,' he coolly suggested, 'just a couple more.'

Amanda blushed suitably, and wished the cameraman well with his scoops of the day.

There were no questions for the couple to answer, yet they had considered it a start. The paper had a morsel to chew on. Next time, they'd announce their engagement.

Indeed, a few days later, they were back. And this time, they arrived together, and sat at the same table.

''82 Claret, sir?'

'Yes please... Well, Amanda, this I think will be the biggy for the media.'

'I believe you're right, Robert. I recognize the guys from The Telegraph over there, and The Daily Mail is out in force, too. Fingers crossed they will have their scoop.'

'Ah, here comes our wine. Thank you, my friend.'

Once they'd ordered the food, they went on talking, a little less stiffly than before. After all, life was fast these days, and most people expected celebrities to lead the way.

'I wouldn't have believed Claridges would allow the press a 'free for all' inside the restaurant. Perhaps they're experimenting with the idea.'

'I shan't hazard a guess how long it will last, Amanda. There are celebrities and celebrities. We are somewhat biased at this point in time, are we not?'

She laughed. It was her first outburst to be heard. One of the cameramen lifted his gaze to their table, and instantly recognized Amanda as the famous fashion designer he'd photographed many times before. She could easily have been a model, but fate had taken a hand and merely granted her wealth and fame as a designer. She had always been happy about that.

'He's coming our way, Robert. Here we go.'

'Hi, Amanda. May we?'

'Of course, Alan. You'll be discreet, I trust?'

'Discreet? You know better than most The Telegraph is always discreet.' He grinned wickedly, snapping away like billy-oh. Amanda swallowed a few memories.

'Lovely, Amanda. You look gorgeous. And who is this handsome gentleman, may I ask? Tom Cruise, himself?'

'At your service.' Robert rose from his seat and bowed graciously. It was clear to the cameraman

173

that 'Tom Cruise' had miraculously grown in the right direction. But Robert was enjoying all this and continued: 'No,' he said, 'not exactly in his league.' As Robert sat down again, Amanda spoke up. She faced Alan the cameraman and announced without embarrassment:

'I don't need Tom Cruise. This man will do me very nicely, thank you.' Cheers and clapping followed and the room waited for more. 'And I'm delighted to announce our engagement to be married.'

'Wow. Congratulations, Amanda, and to you, sir.' Another press-man from The Telegraph wrote on his pad:

FASHION DESIGNER AMANDA ENGAGED TO TOM CRUISE

He reluctantly amended the last name to...

'May we have the lucky gentleman's name, Amanda?'

'Of course. Meet Mr Robert Smythe.'

Robert bowed his head, and then stretching his smile further, clasped Amanda with a kiss.... Click, click, click went the cameras again. 'Congratulations, Mr Smythe. You're a lucky man.'

'Thank you. I think so, too.' He kept smiling. The Telegraph was happy, and the couple sat back once more. 'Shall we bother with The Daily Mail, darling?'

'Oh Robert, don't be such a snob.' He laughed and she laughed with him. They were not to be let off lightly. For The Daily Mail guys had no intention of missing out on the engagement of a celebrity in Claridges.

Click, click, click went the cameras. Another announcement, this time from Robert, beaming his happiness and clasping Amanda's hand over the table; and The Daily Mail had its share of the spoils. Great pictures sell, anyway, but the gorgeous Amanda and her Tom Cruise look-a-like... WOW.

Next day, the story and pictures were splashed across the papers, and tongues predictably wagged. But no one ever remembered Carl Himmler looking like Tom Cruise. Besides, for such a powerful businessman, Carl had, for the most part, maintained a low profile and had rarely been seen in public. More importantly for both Amanda and her Robert, even the faintest suspicion of foul play was just not there. Their fairytale had just begun: all over again.

Chapter 25

It was a huge hurdle cleared, and they thanked their lucky stars they were now free to get on with their lives - in London, in Oxfordshire, anywhere they chose.

The children, Adam and Sally, sang for joy, and Adam gave himself a fright when, in an enthusiastic attempt at a high C in choir practice, his voice disconcertedly dipped to a basso profondo by mistake. Or was it nature taking its course? He reached for his crotch, and searched for those elusive balls, or had they dropped while his attention had been on reaching that bloody high C? Perhaps it was just a warning.

'Time to move on, Adam?' suggested his observant choir-master. 'We're short of basses, as it happens.'

Adam laughed and covered his embarrassment as best he could.

Sally went on practising Mozart during the lovely weekends at the manor with mummy and daddy. She could hardly wait for June 18th.

Meanwhile, Amanda made arrangements for the children to change their surname from Himmler to Smythe by Deed Poll. She had never been in the business of procrastination, unlike others she knew. Time was precious, and life would one day end. What was the point of wasting it unnecessarily? If there is life after death, then logic points to a connection with what one does in this one. If there is no life after death, why squander what is available now? If we live to 100, it is gone all too quickly.

Sure enough, June 18th was upon them before they had time to brood. It was initially thought the wedding should attract the minimum attention from any quarter which could stir up trouble. They had had enough of that 'commodity' to last them a hundred lives. Surely there was a limit to what a human being could be expected to endure?

The Chelsea Registry Office would have been perfectly adequate for the purpose. But Adam, bless him, had suggested Brompton Oratory. After all, he was still a choirboy there, and but for that one awkward moment when even he feared he was turning into a man before his time, he was still respected as a senior boy with musical experience on his side.

Amanda and Robert had listened to Adam's suggestion with interest and agreed to go for it, and damn the risks.

'Great,' exuded young Adam. 'And even if my voice breaks during the ceremony, you'll know it's still your son, won't you?'

''Course we will, darling. We love you, man or boy.'

'Might as well get it over with, Adam. Nature plays funny tricks, sometimes.'

Robert smiled on his son who appreciated the sentiment.

'Well,' resumed the boy unfazed, 'I could make a point of it by coolly moving back a row to the mens' stalls, and joining the basses as if nothing happened?' Robert burst out laughing and gave his son a hug.

'That's my boy.'

Amanda and Sally stood by, watching the two of them joust in good-humoured verbal repartee. It was wonderful to witness: father and son as real pals.

So here they all were: Brompton Oratory on a Saturday afternoon, June 18th. Outside, the sun shone down on London as though it belonged here. The organ was letting rip in a run-up to an extraordinary event. What could be more amazing than a man getting married to the woman to whom he was already wed under another name, and with their son ensconced in the choir-stalls, wondering whether he'd become a man before the service was over or remain a boy for a while longer?

Sally sat in the front row of the congregation with her grandfather. Yes, David Davidson had flown over once more, to attend a new, happy event. He had liked Carl Himmler, and wondered whether Amanda's new man would come up to scratch. He'd had no time to get to know him before today, so he sat with Sally in the pew and looked on, philosophically. He hoped his daughter knew what she was doing. Time would tell. The service began.

Usual stuff... Then a hymn - For All The Saints... No mishap.

The marriage service: the entreaties, priestly warnings... And then came 'any objections': Robert and Amanda held their breath. The moment passed. They relaxed. So did David Davidson who suspected something. But his lips would be sealed, at least for now.

The vows, prayers... An anthem followed. Adam's voice held - just.

Then came another hymn, for all to join in - JERUSALEM - And Did Those Feet in Ancient Times... a magnificent interpretation from choir and organ alike.

The first verse proceeded without a hitch. The Organ interlude followed; then the final verse... and Adam had become a man. As predicted in jest, he wasted no time complaining, but moved with professional ease to the mens' stalls to take up the cudgels in the bass section. The men could indeed do with a boost. With a comical expression on his face, Adam looked down into the nave to his grandfather who grinned in response. It's showbiz, they both seemed to say.

Outside, in bustling Knightsbridge, the press eagerly awaited the happy couple - Amanda and her new man. But The Telegraph and Daily Mail were there first, and waited to catch them as soon as they came out of the Oratory. They crowded the doors... Then suddenly: 'Here they come, lads.' Snap, snap, snap... Wow, what great pictures. 'Blimey,' enthused one excited cameraman, ''e's even betta lookin' than Tom Cruise. And taller.'

At last the party extracted themselves from the press and moved off to the reception: a simple affair, held at the house in Brompton Square. Dembrey opened the door with a rare, beaming face. Luigi had made some delicious little cold dishes, and everything was ready.

None of Robert's family from Hamburg was there, and Amanda quietly thanked those heavenly stars which appeared to be working overtime in her favour. But David Davidson, her father, shook hands warmly with Robert, quickly recognizing the touch, the voice, the vibes. Little could fool David. Yet he kept his counsel, for everyone's sake. There'd be plenty of time for plain, honest truth when the dust had settled. Besides, he believed everyone was entitled to a second chance in life. Who was he to spoil the illusion?

At last, it was over, and with David safely on his way back to New York, the Smythes relaxed in

180

the drawing-room, and cuddled each other. Even Sally seemed to have lost her resentment towards her bright brother, and gave him a special squeeze as if to say 'you will now protect me if I'm in trouble, won't you?' He responded and pulled his sister to his side. She was getting used to his new voice.

There'd be no official honeymoon. What would be the point?

'Let's just stay at the manor for the week, shall we, mummy?'

'Yes, I think that's what we'll do, Sally. We're all pretty tired, anyway. We can relax there, can't we?'

'We can. But if you and daddy really want to get away, don't worry about Adam and me. We can take care of each other, can't we, Adam?'

'That's right, Sally.' Adam's new deep voice boomed out into Sally's ears. She giggled with amusement.

'Because, mummy,' she said, 'he's a man now, isn't he?'

'Yes, dear.'

Chapter 26

The years would roll on - some taking their time, and others flashing by without proper warning as if to prove to the Smythes that they, like any other family, would never be their master.

But they were happy. Little by little, Amanda made improvements to the manor as she saw fit whilst appreciating the house would speak for itself and tell her what needed to be changed. It would always be a joint effort. As for her talks with her daughter, it became obvious that Sally was set on her ambitions as a fashion designer. And why not? Her drawings and designs were showing great maturity as well as flair and imagination. It was decided she should basically remain in London – to attend secondary school and then design college. Her mother would keep an eye on her while giving her all the help and support she would need to achieve her aims. Who knows? Maybe Sally would one day succeed her mother at the boutique and even inherit the house in Brompton Square?

As for Adam, he had already done serious work on that book. And what a story. But would he ever finish it? How would the story end, anyway? And while his desire to study at Oxford remained unshaken he decided he'd embark upon a novel, set in Victorian England. Adam knew in his bones it could hardly compare with his future book about his family. But, to this end, he was prepared to be patient.

Even Amanda sensed there'd be yet more drama in her life with Robert. Maybe it was a vital ingredient - to keep her going, to stimulate, to excite. Anything is preferable to utter boredom. And now this morning – barely a year after her re-marriage - she was feeling a bit queasy. Nothing serious, she trusted. But she rang the doctor for a quick appointment.

In his surgery, the doctor examined the lovely Amanda and made a cheerful announcement:

'Yes, Amanda. Good news, my dear. Nothing to worry about. You're pregnant.'

'Pregnant?'

'You have heard of the condition?'

'But that was years ago. How could this be?'

'Seeing you know not a man, and all that Virgin Mary stuff?' He laughed.

She let go and stopped pretending.

'Well, would you believe it, eh, at my age?'

'Ah, c'mon, my dear. You're not that old. You're still in fine form and you have a handsome, virile husband.'

'That seems to be true, doctor. I suppose I should feel elated?'

'Well, aren't you?' The doctor looked deep into Amanda's eyes and found there an odd mix of surprise and resentment. 'You should be pleased,' he encouraged. 'I'm sure the baby will be both beautiful and healthy. You are alive, my dear. But relax a little more and enjoy yourself. Are you still working?'

'Oh yes, I attend my boutique when I can. I could, of course, hand the general running of the store over to my manageress. She's been doing this on and off for quite a time.'

'There you are, then. Take it easy for a change, Amanda. It's time to pace your life more. You work hard and you do tend to go hell for leather. Am I right?'

'Spot on, doctor. You're a good man. I'll think seriously about your advice.'

'But you won't take it, eh?' He gave her a comical, understanding glance of gentle warning.

'We'll see.'

Robert responded to the news with positive delight and quipped: 'Well, darling, we do tend to go at it hammer and tongs. Are you surprised by the result? It's just wonderful, wonderful.' They embraced. She looked at him with loving, misty eyes and smiled. Accidents will happen, she mused.

It would be a good time to tell the children the news. Adam was here on holiday from school, and Sally also happened to be in the house this morning. Amanda called them to her side and wondered how they'd take it. She decided to keep things on the light side...

'Now, my darlings, I have some news for you. Ready for it?' Adam and Sally stood and waited, wide-eyed. 'Your mother is going to have a baby,' she announced without hesitation.

'Wow, mum, after all this time. But congratulations, anyhow.'

'Thank you, Adam.'

'May I take him out in the pram, mummy?' Rather like The Queen of England, Sally would always address her mother as 'mummy', no matter what age she had reached.

'Yes, Sally. But it won't be for another nine months. He or she has to grow in mummy's tummy, like you and Adam did a while ago.'

'Oh, of course.' Sally could not quite accept her mother's tease.

'Why just 'oh, of course,' Sally? We both know how babies are born.' Adam considered it was time Sally grew up. Amanda smiled on her two children. They really were quite entertaining when ribbing each other as though they were still little kids. But Adam had not finished talking:

'When is the baby expected, mum?'

'In April, I believe. They think the 20th.'

'Oh no.' Adam looked worried.

'What's bothering you, darling?'

'Do you know who was born on 20th April, mum?'

'Millions of babies, I suspect. Who've you in mind?'

'Adolf Hitler.'

'Oh dear. Nevertheless, I doubt my second son, if indeed it is a boy, will ever be allowed to follow in that creature's footsteps, do you?'

'Let's hope not'.

The months passed, and much to Adam's horror, the baby boy indeed entered the world at six-thirty on the evening of 20th April. It was the same calendar date and same hour to the minute of Hitler's birth. A cold shiver passed along Adam's spine on realizing the 'coincidence'. Thankfully Amanda had felt no fear and the minimum of pain. In fact, both Adam and Sally had been more uncomfortable births for her.

For the time being Amanda would remain impervious to superstitions, whilst Robert voiced his delight and smothered his wife and baby with kisses galore.

Sally and Adam looked upon their mother, lying in bed in St. Mary's Hospital, Paddington, and offered their assistance in anything she required of them. Sally had brought a huge bunch of late daffodils, and put them on the bed with love from her and Adam.

'Thank you, my darlings. What would I do without you?'

'You have him, now, mummy.'

'Yes, but I still love you and Adam, Sally, and that means for ever.'

The children kissed their mother, and handed over to dad. Adam tried to bury his unease over the date of the baby's birth. Coincidences occurred in life, so why shouldn't the day and time of birth be as simple as that? Besides, mum appeared to show little interest in studying the Nazi period, anyway. To her mind, it was an aberration of the past - seriously wicked, but the past. Robert had proved that to her, even as Carl Himmler whose name gave her that uncomfortable shiver along her spine when he'd first announced himself in Morton's, how many years ago?

Amanda had kept a beady eye on Adam and Sally while she held the baby in her arms and talked to Robert. She could sense what they were thinking and feeling, and was anxious to reassure them of her love for them.

'Now, come on, you two. I will never cease to love you as I have always done. This 'Tiny Tim' is bound to take more of my attention for a while. You both understand why, don't you?'

'Of course, mum. Sally and I are not kids, any more. By the way, you're not thinking of calling him Tiny Tim?'

Amanda laughed and considered the idea. 'No, dear. How about Peter?'

187

The Smythes put on their thinking caps, while mother cuddled and cooed and her baby gurgled his contentment. The screaming would surely follow, but at least there was no sign of that ridiculous moustache. Adam would have to be thankful for small mercies whilst remaining fearful for the future.

Chapter 27

Amanda got her way: the baby would be called Peter Smythe - not a bad name for a financier, an art dealer, a writer...

'Hey, mum. I shall be the writer in this family. Peter can, well...' Adam searched for suitable words that would not hurt his mother's feelings, whilst voicing his own concern. Or was it plain, old-fashioned jealousy rearing its ugly head?

'Of course you will, darling. But all kinds of things happen in life. Peter will probably stick to finance. He looks a bit like an accountant, already, don't you agree?'

Adam kept his innermost thoughts to himself. 'Boring' would be one of the epithets attached to that profession and, perhaps, to the image expounded by the bundle lying in his mother's arms.

'Maybe he'll be a politician,' continued Amanda. She seemed keen to find her baby something to do before he'd had a chance to be a child.

'We'll see, mum.'

Peter began to cry. He needed changing again, and Amanda's manageress at the boutique had been taken sick. She would love to pop the baby in the pram in his new nappies and wheel him into the shop, and damn the confusion. But she thought better of it. After seeing to the baby, she grabbed her mobile and phoned the shop.

'Ah, Fiona. I'm glad it's you. Are you holding the fort okay?'

'I am, Amanda. Don't worry about a thing. We expect Sheila to be back tomorrow. Something she's eaten, the doctor said. He's given her some pills. We'll cover her. You have plenty to do, I should imagine. How's the little one?'

'Oh, normal, I'd say: happy one minute, screaming his head off the next. And what a scream. I don't think my man Dembrey can take it much longer, bless his cotton socks. He's an old man, now, Fiona - just getting used to an orderly life again, and along comes His Nibs.'

Fiona sympathized as best she could. Lucky bitch, she thought to herself. Pretending to complain when she's sitting on a fortune and pampered by a butler and a cook. Some people have all the luck. 'Oh, it looks as if we have some real customers, Amanda.'

'Don't let me hold you up. Thanks for covering, Fiona. Love to Sheila. 'Bye.'

For once, baby Peter had held his silence while his mother had been on the phone. As she turned her attention to him again, he gave her an extraordinarily cold stare: hard, calculating, cruel, a cut above a 'creative' accountant. The moment passed, the baby cried anew, and Amanda got on with the rituals of motherhood.

How the years rushed by. But that's life, as they say. And while Peter grew and grew, Adam and Sally looked to their own lives and followed their chosen paths.

Sally's drawings began to cause a stir when one of the leading London colleges of design featured a number of her drawings in their new prospectus, and Amanda displayed a few select dresses of her daughter's in the boutique. University was definitely off the cards as far as Sally was concerned, and her mother did not complain. After all, she herself had done extremely well without that particular experience.

Adam, on the other hand, had long been considered university material, and his boyhood desire to go to Oxford which had indeed materialized in the form of a History Scholarship at his great uncle's old college - Lincoln, in The Turl, had brought much delight to his parents, and even Sally had given him a big hug and kiss of congratulation. Moreover, while doing his post-graduate course and earning a meagre living as a junior free-lance journalist he pressed on with writing novels. At least he could improve his technique before publishing 'the biggy'.

'You'll definitely write that book, now, Adam, and get it published. Am I in it?'

'Of course, Sally. I've changed all the names, but no doubt, you'll recognize yourself.' He smiled, and kissed his sweet sister.

Fate, however, would conspire to stay Adam's hand. He somehow sensed his mother would face more distress before her life was over, but he hoped and prayed she would come through it all with fortitude and determination. She was a strong woman, and he wanted to write a book that reflected that strength and his admiration for her, a book that would bring a few genuine tears to the reader, a story that would combine international intrigue with love and compassion.

By the time Peter Smythe had reached his nineteenth birthday, he had grown into a tall, handsome young man with an athletic body and fine, blond hair - a perfect role model for the SS of The Third Reich, exactly as Hitler would prefer all his young men to have looked.

Yet, despite his intelligence, Peter had shown little interest in academic or artistic pursuits. Sport and a certain amount of bullying were another matter. Unfortunately for others, he had been allowed to get away with the latter, when at school he would tower over his victims until they pleaded with him to let them go.

Compounding this behaviour, Peter had resented his brother's neglect of him, or rather his visible aversion. He could not understand why Adam would look through him as though he were either not there or merely another insect to study under the microscope. What had he done to deserve this, apart from pulling the wings off butterflies when he was a small boy, or throwing stones at lovers in the park? And Sally had proved hardly more interested in him, either. Maybe she was afraid of him, as he stood stock still in his boy scout's uniform when he was twelve years old - almost as though he couldn't wait to swap this for a more serious outfit such as the uniform of the SS. Then they'd take notice of him. Then they'd sit up and beg, and tremble with abject fear.

Oh yes, young Peter indeed possessed a morbid interest in The Third Reich and its teachings. His mother had caught him avidly devouring the contents of several publications pertaining to and glorifying The Regime. Though shocked at the time, she said nothing, hoping he would grow out of it.

But Peter continued his pursuit in secret. It was so exciting. Moreover, in one magazine he spotted a pertinent photo of a young SS Officer. Peter realized it was the spitting image of himself. He continued to look at the photo, and smiled, and even kissed the face of the young blond man. Narcissism had got to work in the Smythe household.

Peter had made up his mind. If his family had rejected him, so be it. He would make his own mark in the world, and the world would take notice. He decided to form a gang of like-minded young men and have some fun.

But before he had time to start this process, his father approached him one evening before dinner…

'Sit down for a moment, will you, Peter? I want to have a little chat.'

'What about, dad?'

'Don't get worried. Just relax.'

Peter did as he was told, and sat in a comfortable chair to hear out his father.

'Like a drink?' Peter looked up with surprise. Perhaps it was not going to be as bad as he feared.

'Okay, dad. I'd love a scotch.'

'All right, then. Why not? I'll join you.' Robert walked over to the drinks cabinet, and poured two good measures of Dalwhinnie. He was not sure his son had tried such a good whisky, but maybe the quality would impress the lad and put him at ease in his father's company. Robert returned with the glasses and handed his son his whisky. 'I don't believe you've tried this one, Peter.'

'What is it, dad?'

'Dalwhinnie, a very fine fifteen year-old malt.'

'Wow.' Peter took a sip, and then another. 'Blimey, it's great, dad. Real smooth.'

'Glad you approve. Cheers.'

'Cheers.'

'Now, your mother tells me she's worried about the literature you like to read. Can you enlighten me?'

'How d'you mean? I don't read Shakespeare, or anything like that.'

'No, but I mean books and magazines about the Nazi regime in Germany, for instance?' Robert never liked to beat about the bush, but he believed in civilized interviews.

'Oh dad, most of us at school were interested in that period, as bad as it might seem to the world, now.'

'It's right and, in my opinion, imperative we should study that period in Germany's history, Peter, but it was a shameful period, and we should never forget that.'

'Shameful?'

'Yes, shameful.' Robert took another sip of his whisky, and wished now he'd never begun this conversation. As a German with the name of Himmler, his son would surely pounce on the fact and simply delight in the idea of reviving 'the cause'. Robert held his counsel. He'd had years of practice. And over the last ten to fifteen of them, his accent had further ironed itself into a gorgeous mélange of rich colours but without a trace of German. He felt guilty, hiding his ancestry if not the awesome name of Himmler from his youngest son. But he just had to keep the secret from him. Like Amanda, his beautiful, loving wife, he hoped against hope that Peter's current interest in The

Third Reich and its terrifying agenda would fizzle out and be replaced by a healthy pursuit of the opposite sex. It had done him no harm when he was Peter's age.

'But, father, it was the most exciting period of Germany's history.' Peter would not give up.

'Not so exciting for the millions in the death camps, son'.

Peter's face turned red, not with shame as it might well have done, but with an anxiousness his father might be clever enough to spot that missing ingredient in his son's moral fibre. For Peter had never really felt guilty about anything in his young life. Conveniently, his father mistook the reason for the red face, and turned his attention to the impending family dinner.

Chapter 28

It was indeed a family gathering - rather an extended one, for Adam Smythe, now in his early thirties, had married a girl he'd met at Oxford, and to whom he'd returned after a spell of sowing those proverbial wild oats. Lucky for him she was willing to take him back, but then, she had no doubt been experimenting, too. They already had a son of five, and there was another child on the way. Adam hoped it would be a girl - to follow the pattern of his own childhood. Moreover, his small son, Tom, named after Adam's great-uncle, slept blissfully throughout most of the adult meals. There was no guarantee, of course, how long this extraordinary blessing would last.

And Sally, only a year and a half younger than her brother, had also married – but to her mind a reliable, solid businessman. They had produced two children, named Polly and Graham who had taken it in turns to cry and violate the otherwise tranquil atmosphere of the household. Yet her parents, Amanda and Robert, remained full of love and understanding. They'd seen it all before. Besides, they had produced a third child of their own, a bit of an outsider, a handsome one-off. Or would he for ever be regarded as the black sheep of the family, the woodpecker in the pie?

'Well, Peter. How are you, these days?' Sally had just settled the children upstairs, and was about to join the family for dinner.

'Oh, all right, Sally. Just had a talk with dad. I didn't know he was into whisky. I approve.'

Sally had no idea what Peter was really getting at. But she knew him to be the sly one. She wasn't that blind. And she had the distinct feeling it would behove her to leave it at that, and move on. Her husband, Raymond, would remain a bit of a twerp in Peter's eyes, and those eyes had drifted towards Adam's youthful wife. She was pretty, in an obvious way, but too fidgety – a typical self-conscious school teacher, trying too hard. No class, to Peter's mind. He admired class and brutality - odd bedfellows, perhaps, but qualities ironically possessed by many a successful man or woman.

Then there were his parents - his mother Amanda, and father Robert. Amanda, a beauty, certainly, if one liked that sort of thing; intelligent, confident, practical, loving in a rather overt, Jewish way (I wonder if she'll oppose me? thought Peter. She had certainly gabbed to dad about the magazines). Then finally, there was father - a fine-looking specimen of the Arian race. Take away the beard, and straight into the hot-seat of Head of the SS. What was he waiting for? He had expounded his horror of the death camps. But they were just words, an attempt to control and discipline his younger son and lock him in a cage

198

of boring do-gooders - mamby-pamby folk, clucking away like chickens, and running about in aimless pursuit of normality, only to end up in the mire of mediocrity.

Violence, evil: that's what remained exciting. Peter had no intention of joining the suicide bombers in a hopeless chase after seventy-two virgins. Bugger that lark. Peter would form his own band of thugs - white racists, and play havoc with the system. If the Muslims could do it, why shouldn't he? A bit more violence to stir the blood. If his father only knew...

The dinner went off without a hitch, much to the relief of Robert and Amanda. And for a change, many hands made light work, and no one seemed to get in anyone's way. Old Dembrey had long gone - passing away in his sleep over ten years before, having lifted that very day his last dram of whisky to the lips with an apt comment: 'Beautiful. I've had enough'. Luigi, on the other hand, was still a comparatively young man, and had never lost his magic touch in the kitchen. Amanda had remained loyal to him, and he to her. She thanked those stars again that Italian doesn't necessarily mean unfaithful.

Sally's dress designs had become as famous as her mother's in her day. Fashions would come and go, but old favourites would survive. Black would never die, but only certain women could show it off for its elegance. Sally's husband was also earning good money - in The City, and had bought a house in Knightsbridge that would, he hoped, facilitate Sally's work in the area. It would soon be time, moreover, for Sally to take over the running of her mother's boutique. As for the house in which they were dining in Brompton Square, who knows? Early days, they supposed.

Adam sat back in his chair after dinner, with a cigar and cognac, and surveyed the fascinating scene before him. No novel, he mused, could ever quite match life's unimaginable twists and turns, ironies, idiocies, loves and hates. Here was his extraordinary father, sitting next to him - a man who had taken on more work, pressures and responsibilities than most men could cope with, and come out of it all with strength and love for his family unsurpassed. Adam would never ever betray his dear father, despite the temptations, for he knew his job now as a successful free-lance journalist would open the right doors for him. Yes, he could publish books: he'd already released three novels - political satires that had been well received with glowing reviews. But his biggy, the one about his own family, would have to wait until he himself was entirely satisfied he had covered all angles. A promise is a promise. His family came first, before making a cheap buck.

Peter, thank God, had held both his temper and his tongue over dinner. It was quite an achievement, and Robert wondered whether he could risk having another chat with the boy, with or without the whisky. He felt duty bound to warn off his son from pursuing such a dangerous course of violence that could only end up with a prison sentence or worse. Balancing this duty was the absolute necessity of maintaining secrecy of the Himmler Affair. To Robert's mind, Peter could, if he were persistent or interested enough, dig out the story of Carl Himmler's funeral, and his replacement as Head of TKH Enterprises by another man. But what would that tell him of the real character of his father? And if Robert, in his anxiousness to save the boy from bringing ruin upon himself and others, told him the facts about his past, how could there be any guarantee his son would change his ways?

Robert sat, brooding for a moment or two, until Amanda spotted his change of mood, and quickly steered his thoughts elsewhere.

'Cheer up, Robert. Our family is expanding. It was bound to happen some day, and perhaps if we're nice to them, they'll look after us in our old-age.'

'You think so, darling?'

Peter had had enough. He'd held on to his patience for far too long. This domestic dribble was getting him down. What he needed was action or at least a step towards it. He'd made up his mind.

'Okay, folks. I bid you all goodnight, and...' He was already on his feet.

'Where are you off to, Peter?'

Amanda could hardly hide her anxiousness and disappointment in Peter's attitude, but she knew better than to push him too hard.

'I promised to meet a pal in The Victoria, mum. I won't be late back.'

'All right, Peter. Watch the drinking if you're taking the car.'

'No, I'll take a cab. Don't worry, mum. I may still be a youngster, but I don't hang out in discos, pumping drugs. A pint or two and a whisky will do me. Don't worry.'

Everyone bid goodnight to Peter, and the lad was let loose. He took a cab to The Victoria pub, on the other side of the park, as he said he'd do, there to begin the process of forming or at least joining a gang of like-minded guys. The British National Party would never satisfy him - dressing up in suits and ties and trying to convince the media that they were not racist, after all.

Chapter 29

Much to Peter's delight and satisfaction, his friend Mark Stranger was already leaning over the bar of The Victoria, ordering a couple of pints, one for Peter and one for himself.

Like Smythe the younger, Mark Stranger admired efficiency and people who arrived on time for appointments. This evening could be the start of something big. The country needed a good shake-up. It had become too soft, too mamby-pamby, too tolerant of foreigners, especially those who had the audacity to upset the delicate balance of the British way of life. The British National Party had indeed had a shot at changing things, but it had got nowhere. Having escaped a few court cases by the skin of its teeth, its activities would for ever be monitored and controlled by the establishment, such as it was. Besides, to Mark's warped mind, no one was having any fun these days. 'Happy Slapping' was kid's stuff. Where was the beef, the organization?

'Well, Peter, let's begin with a pint apiece.'

'Thanks, Mark.' They drank to 'The Cause'.

'But let's get one thing straight. The leadership of this gang. You say you want to be the boss. But I have the experience. I also enjoy the rough stuff, get my drift?' Mark stared Peter in the face with the hint of a smirk. Peter held his ground, and Mark appeared impressed.

'You've got the image, I must say,' continued Mark, 'a good-looking SS type to a tee. I'm more yer bully-boy. But what would A.H. have done without 'em, eh?'

'I assume you refer to Adolf Hitler?'

''Course. Now, Peter, what d'you say? Do you agree I should be leader, or do we fight over it?'

Peter thought on his feet, and agreed that considering Mark's experience in the BNP, in other right-wing gangs, The National Front and so on, he must have learned something, if only how not to do things.

'Well, Mark, perhaps I'm a bit too young for the job at the moment, but just watch this space.'

Mark laughed. He was getting to like this young man in front of him, and felt sure he could lick him into shape. Metaphorically speaking, of course.

Back at the house in Brompton Square, the family discussed the latest crisis to hit them - the behaviour and mental condition of the young, rebellious Peter.

'What's really bothering you, dad?' asked Adam, concerned his father had been through enough trouble to warrant problems with a young, errant son.

'Your mother found him with his head buried in Nazi literature, or at any rate literature propagating and glorifying the Nazi ethos.'

Judging by Peter's awkward, self-conscious behaviour over the years, Adam was hardly surprised by his father's revelation. But he kept quiet and allowed him to release and expand on his anxiousness.

'So,' continued Robert, 'I decided to have a man to man talk with him, in a nice way over a glass of whisky.'

'Go on,' said Adam, taking mental notes and thinking how sad it was that Peter could not properly appreciate his father's kindness and good nature.

'It seemed to me he had no sense of shame for that loathsome regime, but simply gloried in its teachings and activities. I confess I am stumped as to what I should do about him. If only he showed an interest in girls, it might cure him of this morbid pursuit.'

'Perhaps he prefers boys,' offered Sally, complicating matters further. Robert reached for his whisky.

'Possible,' acknowledged Amanda philosophically. 'He's a good-looking boy, and bound to attract the interest of both sexes.'

'Well, he hasn't shown much interest in either, to our knowledge, Amanda. So he could be a dark horse, or...' Robert failed to complete his thesis.

'Closet Queen?' Adam's wife Jill added her contribution to the current crisis.

'Whatever his problem,' said Robert, sensing he should wrap up this inquest into his younger son's condition, 'I mean to get to the bottom of it.'

'Oo,' exclaimed Adam with a smile and imitation of one of his gay friends he'd known at Oxford. He couldn't resist the tease; and even his father laughed. It certainly lightened the atmosphere, and everyone called for another drink.

Newly refreshed, they all braced themselves for Peter's return before midnight. But, with another whisky to bolster him, Robert felt strong enough to reopen the discussion about Peter before laying it to rest. With his family there, he could let go, and empty himself of this worry without delay. At any rate, that was his theory.

'Seriously,' he went on, 'for once in my life, I'm stumped. What do you think, darling?' He turned to Amanda as the last and dependable resort in his hour of indecision. 'Surely you know what to do?'

Silence prevailed as all eyes focused on Amanda, the steady one, the beautiful bulwark of the tribe, the reasonable and caring woman who would know the answer to any human problem, especially in her own family...

'No,' she responded faintly, her lovely face wearing an expression of wistful longing for a life, less complicated, less frustrating.

They sat for a while in extraordinary silence as though waiting for a sign, a spiritual message from beyond that would galvanize them into action, an action that was supposed to resolve the current difficulty. But no sign was forthcoming, no ghost, no voice from beyond or within them except a small voice of resignation: What will be will be – Qué sera, sera.

Robert slumped impotently in his chair. He'd never experienced the condition physically, thank God, but the mental version was probably as bad, if not worse. Should he have Peter locked up? Should he call his friend Arthur Biggs, long retired from the service and now Lord Biggs, to seek advice - only to open a can of worms and risk danger of unwanted publicity and confusion?

Oh God, if I pray hard enough, maybe the problem will go away. And maybe Peter will meet a girl or even a boy who will divert his attention from fascism and bring the lad back into a world of joy and love. Anything to prevent a catastrophe.

They were still sitting there when a key turned in the front door. Peter had come home, looking quite pleased with himself and happy to talk. 'Hi, folks.'

'Hi, Peter. Had a good time?' Robert put away his worry lines and smiled.

'Yes thanks, dad. Just a change of scenery, you know. Have you a coffee, mum?'

'Of course, dear. We'll all have one, shall we, folks?'

They moved to the drawing-room to sit down in comfortable sofas and chairs, and perhaps watch a spot of television while they drank coffee.

Amanda soon made the beverages and brought in the cups on a wheeled coffee-table. She added a few tempting biscuits for those with a sweet tooth.

Even Peter stayed to join in the family circle. He'd had his break: not exactly a night on the tiles, but at least a break from the perceived life of the bourgeoisie.

Adam turned on the television. And there, staring at them in the room was the elated face of an infamous dictator. It was a repeat of a BBC documentary entitled 'The Fatal Attraction of Adolf Hitler'.

'Just what the doctor ordered,' quipped Robert unbelievingly. How cruel could fate be to him, when he was trying to do his best for his younger son?

'That's all we need,' added Raymond, Sally's husband whose Jewish family had been in finance for generations.

'I dare say, Peter, this is right up your street?' Robert shot his son an uncomfortable stare. But Peter shrugged his shoulders. He was not about to deny his interest in the subject. Why should he? After his talk with his father?

'Yes, father. I'd like to watch this. In fact, I think we all should - if only to give us an insight into the conditions at the time.'

Several members of the family were itching to speak out, but Robert quietly hushed them to allow Peter his say. It was better for all this to be in the open, rather than screwed up inside the lad. They obliged, and Peter continued. 'We will then understand a little more of why Hitler did what he did.'

'Oh,' replied Raymond cynically. He wanted to go home, but Sally nudged him into staying. At least the coffee and biscuits might help.

As the programme proceeded, the family dissents gradually diminished and they were irresistibly drawn to the screen. The presenter from Cambridge was doing a good job, and the BBC had pieced the story together with consummate skill. Many famous personages appeared to explain how reasonable it all seemed, including Lord Bullock, the historian whose knowledge of that period had hardly been surpassed. Anthony Eden appeared, relating how he met Hitler after The First World War. Then there was Lloyd George, and the filming of his visit to Hitler's retreat where he was given high tea, served by The Fuehrer's special officers. Lloyd George congratulated the dictator on restoring Germany's honour... And on it went, until the turning point when Germany lost her innocence: The Night of the Broken Glass, the hounding of the Jews, the bombing of Poland, war against Russia and the death camps...

'Stop it,' shouted Raymond from his chair. 'Stop this nonsense. I don't want to see any more of that bastard. I hope he's burning in hell. Come on, Sally. We're going. Thank you, Amanda, thank you Robert... I think,' he said, lowering his voice, 'you have a problem on your hands, Robert. I don't envy you, my friend. Keep in touch.'

'Thanks for coming, Raymond. And you, Sally, dear. Look, don't disturb the kids right now. Come back in the morning, and pick them up. Good idea?'

'Good idea. Thanks, daddy. And thank you, mummy.'

'It's a pleasure, darling. You take care. See you in the morning.'

When Sally and Raymond had departed, the room calmed down, and the family resumed watching the programme to the end. Hitler's secretary impressed everyone. She seemed such a lovely woman. Could she be expected to know what her boss was really up to?

'Well, Peter. I hope you don't think you can copy what Hitler got away with for a while?'

'No chance, I'm afraid, dad. I'll have to be satisfied with conquering England.'

The whole room sat up, and trusted Peter was only joking and that he would never forget the pathetic end to Hitler's terrifying and misguided life.

Chapter 30

As the following week progressed, family affairs appeared to settle into a comfortable pattern. Adam and his wife Jill and young son Tom had returned to Oxfordshire where they happily lodged in a wing of Amanda's manor. It was a spacious conversion and as elegant as the main house. Jill was a maths teacher at a local school, and Adam worked on his books in blissful contentment, encompassed by English history. It was good to be home.

Sally had already begun her new job, running her mother's boutique, albeit part-time. She thanked God she had a nanny to take the strain with the kids; whilst Raymond, her husband, tried to put the BBC documentary out of his mind. Ironically, it merely served as an incentive for him to make even more money. Two fingers to Hitler and his embittered mind!

As for Peter, his parents continued to monitor his words, actions and general demeanour about the place while jointly deciding to cheer things up: they suggested a holiday for all three of them. They'd then have a relaxed opportunity to get to the truth about their young son without leaning on him too hard, and driving an irretrievable wedge between them. It could be an easy exercise, or it might be difficult or even impossible. Worth a try, they thought.

Somewhat to their disappointment Peter turned down the holiday idea, not brusquely but firmly, saying he'd too much to sort out for himself at the moment. Both Amanda and Robert took that to mean a turn for the better. The boy even said he intended going for an interview for another job, this time in a well-known computer shop in the area. But was he telling the truth?

Amanda continued to worry, despite the fact all had been "quiet on The Western Front" for some time. But then one morning, 44, Brompton Square became the scene of unimaginable horror...

Robert had gone for a walk and the daily paper, leaving Amanda alone in the house with Peter. Amanda finally flipped. Mother and son had just had a blazing row in the course of which Amanda harangued Peter over his rude manners, his lack of appreciation for kindness shown to him by both her and Robert, his father; his cutting, cruel, murderous looks which had not gone unnoticed, his...

'I'm going to my room,' he shouted angrily.

'Good idea,' she bit back. It had become the shouting match she had hoped could be avoided, and neither of them could see how peace would ever be re-established in the house again. The difference was that Peter had every intention of doing his worst. He remained a calculating sod, to say the least.

He ran up to his bedroom, banging shut the door behind him. Determinedly, he opened his wardrobe door, and extracted the SS uniform he'd bought for himself a week ago and had hidden inside a covering zip-bag. He unzipped the bag and retrieved his uniform. God, how he loved it. The sight of it was giving him a hard-on. He slipped into the uniform. Fitted him like a glove. He tightened his belt and put on the terrifying-looking cap. His flies were still open and he was doing the Nazi salute in his full-length mirror when the door opened, and there stood his mother, intending to reason with her son. But her face of utter horror and disgust stirred his anger and resolve:

'Get out, Jew, or else!' Amanda recovered herself and rushed into the room, slapping his face hard:

'How dare you!'

Peter's eyes blazed from his crimson face. He pushed her on to his bed, and began ripping off her clothes. He was still hard, his penis now pushing its way out of his flies. She gasped in horror and fear as he reached for her neck to strangle the noise while he forced his penis into her vagina and began thrusting - forward, back, forward... She still struggled, trying to get her breath, to no avail. He was so strong. He was having his way, this beautiful beast of a son, this rampant ram, this incestuous criminal. The utter horror of it all, the terror... The Iron Cross on his uniform bounced back and forth before her eyes as she imagined him in the form of a handsome yet monstrous SS officer in Auschwitz, forcing her to have sex as his just reward for heavy war duties... And then an American paperback novel flashed through her mind of a little boy, changed by his runaway hormones into a man, penetrating his own mother - until the mother is rushed into a nursing-home and put under heavy sedation. But Peter was already a man, and still on top of her, and still thrusting away... She thought of the incestuous tribes of Africa, South America, even the goings-on in East London 'rabbit-hutches' and Andalucian villages of anarchic Spain, anything to justify this horror and stop herself going mad. She dare not imagine the normality of her boutique right now, so near and yet so far: her own daughter Sally in her element, showing customers the latest of her designs and those of her mother. She dare not think of Harrod's, just over the way across the road, and the customers gleefully ordering this and that; the elegance of it all, the style... while she, Amanda, is being raped by her own young son. "Oh, it's normal, my dear. He'll grow out of it, in time". Thank God Amanda had an imagination to save her. Peter had stopped squeezing her neck, and she took the opportunity to scream and scream, and... He started to hit her, and then... They could hear the front door bang shut, and footsteps rushing up the stairs, and a loud voice: 'Amanda, where are you?' Robert entered the room and took in the scene:

'For God's sake, what's going on? Amanda, darling. Oh my God.' She was shaking and crying and reached for his comforting arms. He hugged her lovingly, ignoring the mess, and then turned to his wicked son, spent it seemed, not only in violent sex but in... could it be shame? Or was the wretched boy faking? Who could ever trust him?

'Right, you. Phone for an ambulance, quickly. Use my mobile, and here's the number.'

Robert had extracted the mobile from his trouser pocket. He always kept it with him, for emergencies. Peter did as he was told, and shakily dialled the number while Robert calmed his wife as best he could. The ambulance arrived in six minutes, and the men were let in by Robert who led the way. He explained as simply as he could without divulging the real facts as he saw them. The hospital, no doubt, would soon discover the horrid truth. Amanda and Robert agreed to persuade the authorities to keep the story out of the papers if they possibly could.

The men gently carried Amanda down the stairs to take her to St. George's Hospital, Hyde Park. She would have rest and care without visitors except her husband. She had urged Robert to stay in the house for a while to deal with Peter.

216

He agreed to her request, and despite her frightful ordeal, she hoped he wouldn't mess it up and cause the boy to do any more damage. But then, who could tell?

With Amanda in safe hands, Robert concentrated on the tricky job of dealing with his son.

Down the stairs they stomped, into the drawing room, and... oh, this was going to be the most difficult job in Robert's life. He knew he was bound to foul it up, but what the hell? He'd had enough trouble: no more, he said to himself. He'd give the boy one last chance, but that was it. He still wished he could divulge his past to Peter if it would do any good. But there was no guarantee of that, and the revelation might make matters even worse. No, he must concentrate on Peter's outrageous, unforgivable behaviour and act of violence and violation.

'Right, Peter. Sit down. Now, you may think me a fool for being so considerate at a time like this, but I am going to offer you a drink to calm you. I myself need one. And maybe, just maybe we can work out a solution to our relationship.'

'That's very generous of you, dad. Have you a Dalwhinnie?'

'I thought you might ask for that. Ah well, in for a penny, in for a pound.' Robert walked over to the cabinet, and poured two stiff Dalwhinnies. He hoped to God the whisky would bring him assistance.

They raised their glasses with grave embarrassment. It seemed a ridiculous situation. Perhaps only men could do this sort of thing with any degree of ease, thought Robert. Women are so emotional and vindictive. It would be understandable. Robert wasn't the one who'd been raped.

'Okay, Peter. Here goes.' He observed his son's control of his own emotions, and was even a little envious. He could not quite do the same. But then, Robert's agenda was not the same. He was dealing with evil here, evil shining from his own flesh and blood, evil that others would have exterminated long before it got to this stage. He tried afresh. 'Now, it's obvious to me what happened in that bedroom of yours. I'm not that stupid. And I'm very angry. But I know your mother to be an extraordinarily tolerant woman who would not want me to lay into you in a physical way. In any case, you'd probably win.'

They raised their glasses with a sip and shade of a smile. 'However, I remain determined to extract your cooperation. Are you listening, Peter?'

'Yes, father. Go on.'

'Your brother Adam and sister Sally have given your mother and me no trouble at all, and have shown their appreciation for our love and care for them in every way. They are both a credit to us. As for you...' Robert hesitated, hoping Peter would do the decent thing and apologize, offer a confession, something to mitigate his disgraceful behaviour. But...

'Okay, dad. Spit it out. What d'you intend doing?'

'That will depend on your co-operation from now on.'

'Co-operation?'

'Yes, you bloody well know the meaning of that word. Come off it, son. You're not that thick. You owe us, Peter. If you want out, get out!'

Peter's eyes bulged in surprise. But then anger took hold of him...

'You are throwing out your own son?'

'Behave and fit into society, Peter, or fuck off.' It was the first time Peter had heard his father use the 'F' word. It was the fact he used it so rarely that made it effective. It stunned Peter for a moment, and even Robert seemed disturbed by his own verbal venom. He wished he possessed the subtlety and way with words that Amanda had. But the words were out, and Peter took advantage. 'Right,' he simply said. He threw his whisky glass into the grate, smashing it into pieces. He stood up, and with a click of his heels and raising his arm, gave the Nazi salute, and stormed out of the room. 'You will regret this,' he shouted over his shoulder, slamming the front door behind him.

Robert had had every intention of making his son take off that ridiculous Nazi uniform, before talking to him. But he figured a fair discussion might lead to Peter volunteering. It led to the opposite path. But then, there remained a good chance he would not get very far in Knightsbridge unless, of course, he caught a Jewish cab to a gay pub in Earls Court. Oh, the madness of life. He finished his whisky and phoned the hospital.

Chapter 31

He was quickly put through to Amanda, who was anxious to speak with him. She had requested not to be sedated. She was a strong woman, she said, but needed to talk and be with Robert, her husband. Her wishes were duly respected, and Robert was soon on his way to St. George's Hospital…

'My darling Amanda.'

'Robert. Thanks for coming here so soon. They've cleaned me up and examined me, and… How did you get on with Peter?'

'Not so fast, darling. Take it easy. You've had a terrible shock. I'm here to comfort you.' He kissed her, and she smiled her love. What would she do without him? She needed him more than ever, now this awful act of violation had been committed by her own son - the latecomer, the one who had given her that strange, cold look when he was still in his pram. Adam had been right. He knew she would somehow go through another trauma before long. He just had to write that book, and she wanted him to do it, to tell the world a real, dramatic, incredible story that would grip the imagination. Whether they believed it or not made no difference. She knew the truth.

The doctor arrived at the bedside to give his verdict. 'You know what happened, I presume, Mr Smythe?'

'I'm afraid I do, doctor. But she looks remarkably fit, considering the outrage upon her.

'Your wife is a strong lady, Mr Smythe. After such an attack, most women would be under heavy sedation and then in need of psychiatric treatment. I sense you two are perfectly capable of returning to normality without our meddling assistance.' The doctor shot Robert a wry smile, much appreciated. Amanda agreed with the doctor's thoughts and requested she be released in order to return to the house with Robert. She promised to phone if there were any residual or subsequent problems. She felt better already, she said. All she wanted was to be with Robert.

'Well, Amanda, you have made your case very firmly and I must say, in all my years as a doctor I have never seen such a resilient patient as your good self. If you'd be so kind as to sign this release form; you too, Mr Smythe, I'll inform staff nurse, and you can be on your way.'

'Thank you, doctor. Er, what d'we owe you?'

'Nothing. You're still on BUPA?'

'Yes.'

'Fine. Well, Amanda, I do wish you all best wishes. Take it easy for a while. Your daughter is running the boutique, they tell me.'

'That's right. She's doing a great job there, and she's well-liked by all the staff.'

'So there, you can treat yourself to a well-earned break, with this man.' The doctor smiled, and caught the whiff of real love between them.

Peter strode determinedly along Knightsbridge, in search of a cab to take him to a friend's house. He'd grabbed his own mobile when his father wasn't looking, and popped it in his trouser pocket. He wanted nothing to spoil the effect of his dramatic departure from Brompton Square. He was on a mission. After phoning his friend, another 'Nazi in waiting' who agreed to his surprise visit, he kept his eyes open for a cab. One taxi-driver gave him a suitable two-finger sign with great aplomb and drove on. Another scowled at him, driving on into the traffic. At last a taxi stopped, and with a broad grin across his face, the driver asked: 'Going to a party, mate? Jump in.'

Peter got in the back of the taxi, and gave his destination to the driver who wanted to talk more about Peter's fancy dress. But Peter was in no mood. It was no laughing matter to him, and this Jew-boy in the driving-seat better watch his tongue if he knew what was good for him.

The cab drew up to the house in South Kensington. It was not Mark Stranger's place, but that of Ian Broad, another tough guy who had supplied Peter his uniform and who had a stock of them in his back room. Peter stepped out of the taxi, and gave the driver the correct money.

'Oi! Where's my tip, then?'

'I don't tip Jews. You have enough money there.' Peter strode off with a host of stinging remarks in his ears: 'That's the thanks I get for picking up a bleedin' Nazi... We fough' two bleedin' wars to get rid of you bastards!'

At last the taxi drove off, and Peter rang Ian Broad's bell.

'Ah, Peter. Come in. You look stunning, my friend. You could go anywhere in that.'

'No time for jokes, Ian. Can we talk?'

'Yes, of course. In here.' Ian led the way through the house and into his back room, stuffed with memorabilia, books, photos and uniforms - the biggest stock of Third Reich paraphernalia in the UK. The guns and live ammunition were wisely kept in a locked cupboard. But it was all the real McCoy. Peter was impressed. He'd collected his uniform by hand in a pub, not from this house.

'Have a seat, Peter.'

They sat down in old, worn leather armchairs that lent a certain club feel to an otherwise nauseous, messy room. 'Can I get you a drink?' offered Ian, politely.

'No thanks, Ian. Not at the moment.'

'Okay. Fire away.'

'Right. How about a real raid on one of the gay pubs in Earl's Court, tonight?' Both young men's faces lit up with the thought of holding-up all those guys, half-dressed in SS uniforms, with their limp wrists and lisping voices, suddenly speechless in fear.

'Wow. What a gig.' Ian had caught on to the idea with enthusiasm. What was the point of all these uniforms, sitting here, waiting for customers who only make a travesty of the whole thing? Why not use them for real, and put some beef into the process?

'Okay, Peter. I'll get on to the guys right away and we'll organize it for a 10.p.m. raid. What d'you say?'

'Great. Now, I'm the boss, Ian. We spread out when we get in there, and line 'em up against the walls. And I want real guns, Ian. Live ammunition, at least for me.'

'Blimey, you're serious.'

'You bet I'm serious. Who are the fellas who'd go through with it?'

Ian put on his thinking cap.

'Ah yes, I've got just the right guys for this operation, Peter.' He grabbed his black book which contained pretty serious but 'sophisticated' thugs who'd love all this. 'We have to have enough of 'em to put the shits up the gays.'

Peter laughed. It was the first time in weeks, it seemed. His family were nice, but too bloody nice. Excitement was what he craved: excitement and danger. It was a straight tunnel for Peter, and he was heading straight for it.

225

His friend Ian called his men on his mobile phone, and put the plan to them. All expressed great interest in doing it, but two said it would be impossible tonight. So, it was down to ten guys. Peter nodded for Ian to fix it. Ian suggested they all met in his house at 6 p.m. Wash and brush up, into uniforms, eat a take-away here which Ian would organize. Discussion of plan 8-9 p.m. to cover timing of entrance to pub, strategy for dealing with the customers, exit plan, etc.

'We can use my big transit van, Peter. We'll all get in there, and I'll drive. I'm a good get¬away bastard. I think you'll be impressed.'

Peter smiled and said he was ready for that drink now.

Meanwhile, Amanda and Robert had returned to Brompton Square to have lunch at home and discuss the whereabouts and possible fate of their errant son, Peter. Luigi was still on vacation, so they'd have to cook for themselves.

'I'll do it, darling. You just rest in the drawing room.'

'No, Robert, I need to keep active for a while. It'll keep my mind off certain... things.'

'Oh, my darling Amanda. You've been through hell. I'm so proud of you. And I love you.' They kissed and held each other. It was a loving, human embrace beyond measure: supreme, unconditional love.

'I'm proud of you, too, my darling man.'

Professional cynics could go to hell. Here were two intelligent people, husband and wife, a German and a Jewess, bound in love - for better or for worse. The 'better' had certainly been good, the 'worse' had been bad. The luck of the draw was theirs to assess. They liked each other - a perfect marriage, as rare and magical as God himself.

Chapter 32

The young men congregated in Ian's house, and after the initial horseplay and fooling around, they settled down to 'serious business'. They were here for a purpose. Peter was soon appointed the spokesman and leader. He was not only very handsome, looking the part in his sparkling uniform, but he remained the most articulate among them. He was a natural leader, though his naivety had yet to be exposed.

Ian proved to be a wizard. He had found a uniform to fit each guy. And then out came the holsters. 'Blimey. Are we really gonna 'ave guns for this party?'

'Wait a minute, wait a minute,' urged Peter over the noise. They all stopped jabbering, and listened. He had the looks. He had the authority. 'Hand up anyone who's too scared to use a gun?' No one put up his hand. Who would confess to be the first to chicken out?' But silence prevailed, and Peter stood up to his full height and looked at them, one by one. Could he bend these guys, most of them older and more brutish-looking than he? Could he bend them to his will as Adolf Hitler had done with his people in his time?

One brave fella spoke out, saying: 'Look, I don't wanna spoil anyone's fun, but let's be realistic. We can't go barging in there with guns blazing and expect to get away scot- free. I thought we were jest gonna stir the old blood and give the queers a fright...'

'We will,' said Peter firmly, 'if we do things my way. We must remain cool about this. My way will terrify them. Are you listening?'

'Yes, Peter. Go ahead.'

He outlined his plan which would result in the customers being lined up, facing the walls. He would be responsible for shooting into the ceiling to achieve this if they did not obey his instructions quickly enough (he was in fact prepared to go further, but kept quiet about it)...

'Then we order drinks all round, I suppose, and tell 'em it was only a prank?' Another brave fella had chanced his arm in the serious company of Peter. But much to everyone's surprise, Peter picked up on the idea.

'Wait a minute. I think you have something there, George. This could be our 'get-out' clause, if you see what I mean.'

'Not if you shoot someone dead.'

'Leave that eventuality to me, George. I take full responsibility.

'Okay by me.''

'And me.'

'Likewise.'

They went on discussing the possibilities, the risks, the fun they could have and even drinks 'on the house', with no hard feelings either side - if they made it up to the gays. Everyone could have some fun before the police arrived. By then the "Old Bill" would no longer be necessary. Or would it give them yet another excuse to stop the carnival?

After a simple home lunch of steak and salad with a good bottle of Burgundy, Amanda and Robert had sat in the drawing room and considered the possibility of Peter phoning some time in the day to say how truly sorry he was for the whole thing, for his utterly ruthless, disgraceful behaviour, his selfishness: everything. But this would be too much to expect him to do. They had to consider he was too far gone: too evil, irredeemable. They were both mature enough to forgive, to try to understand, to bring him back into the fold, into the warmth of a loving family. But if he had chosen another path and had decided he would tread it, what could they do to prevent an inevitable tragedy?

'Well,' concluded Robert with a sigh, 'we could hang around here in the hope he will phone. But my darling, I don't want you to distress yourself further. Even if he doesn't appear tonight, I still don't think we should worry. With that ridiculous uniform and his good looks, someone is bound to offer him a bed for the night, and bring him out of his 'shell'.' He grinned wickedly, and Amanda laughed. It was the first time she'd allowed herself that pleasure since her traumatic experience earlier in the day. She needed to unwind and take her mind off the shock and horror of it all. Think positive, she told herself. I have Robert, my loving husband here with me. If I lose one of my flock, I still have Adam and Sally. True, they each had their own family to look after, now. But they would perpetuate the genes. Robert apart, they are the blessings of my life, she mused. I hope and pray it is all for the best.

At 9.30 p.m., the guys were ready for the fray. One last check of the plan, and 'over the top'. At 9.45 they walked out of Ian's house and piled into the transit. They checked their watches and pistols. Most had rubber bullets (Peter had finally relented in order to keep his 'troops' on his side), but Peter's pistol and those of two other fellas were loaded with live ammunition. Peter had picked two guys as most likely to be responsible and courageous if it came to any necessary shooting. Discipline would be maintained at all times.

Off they zoomed and were soon in spitting distance of the pub. Ian was lucky to find a nearby available meter, and after parking the van he fed it sufficient money before returning to his driving-seat for a fast get-away. Out climbed the other guys, quickly lining up in formation. They marched smartly down the road, and with Peter leading, entered the pub. One of the gang immediately disconnected the jukebox, the others pushing their way to the counter as if to order drinks. They turned and brandished their guns, and with Peter's clear voice cutting through the confused hubbub, the pub fell silent with apprehension and fear. Peter was elated but remained cool... 'Okay, you guys. Face the walls. Now. C'mon, C'mon.' Much to Peter's naive surprise, the gays were loath to be hurried against their will. He had to make a rapid decision. 'All right, you obey, or else...' He quickly fired a shot into the ceiling, creating a hell of a racket and jolting the customers into morose silence. They could not believe it. Here was this gorgeous-looking guy in all the gear, acting like a Nazi thug instead of relaxing, having a good time and jumping into someone's ready bed. He'd have so many offers.

The gays unwillingly turned to face the wall and do what this young idiot told them to do.

Meanwhile, the pub manager had phoned the police, and requested quick action with armed officers. They were on their way.

The gang had spread out and had covered the customers at gunpoint. No one was about to ask politely whether any particular pistol was loaded or not. After seeing the damage Peter had caused with his weapon, they wisely thought it prudent to obey instructions, hoping they would soon be released from this outrageous interruption to their evening.

'What d'you want?' asked one brave guy, a tall American who'd been eyeing Peter as soon as he'd entered the pub. 'You can have me anytime you wish, honey.' People laughed.

'Shut up,' shouted Peter angrily, and the disappointed American turned back to face the wall. The laughter ceased and then the police arrived.

'All right, you lads. Drop the guns. Now.' There were more than a dozen armed policemen. The Chief Officer was a burly brute whose men had no difficulty in disarming Peter's gang, but...'Okay, son. Let me have that.'

Peter faced the officer who kept coming closer. Appearing unarmed, he was covered by other armed men who'd taken aim on the recalcitrant young man in their sights.

'Get back,' shouted Peter, now with a discernible quiver in his voice, as he began to panic. 'Get back or I'll shoot. This is loaded, and I will shoot you. I warn you, get back, get back.'

But the officer kept coming; he was getting closer and closer. Peter's panic was reaching its peak as he croaked his last warning: 'Get back, you fool... All right, you asked for it.' And taking remarkable aim, he fired into the policeman's body. The officer fell instantly, and Peter turned his gun on the other men taking determined aim on him. He hadn't a chance. They were not about to take any more risks with this young bastard.

One shot killed Peter. He fell to the floor with a fearful thud. The police took the rest of Peter's gang into custody. A number of guys cynically noted the transit van had disappeared with Ian in it! The lone American looked down on Peter's body with a predictable but genuine lament: 'What a waste.'

Chapter 33

By 10.30 p.m., it was all over. But in the drawing-room of 44, Brompton Square, Amanda and Robert sat, digesting their second substantial meal of the day. Amanda had made a tasty lamb casserole with peppers and carrots. They still had a few bottles of Nuits St. George in the cellar, and decided tonight of all nights should be the time to relax and listen to some classical music on their CD player. Sod the world. They had had many blessings bestowed upon them. Equally, they'd had their fill of drama and serious trouble. As for Amanda, today had been a day when most women would have cracked up completely. But she had recovered with remarkable speed from her young son's outrage upon her. And now that she had rejoined her husband, she intended to share with him all the love she could pluck from the depths of her soul. Robert was a lovely man - intelligent, complex, but like her, with an enormous capacity for survival and compassion. Having endured the terrors of the morning, she would not sleep again until she'd been brought back to sanity and security. Robert was the one person in the world who could do this for her, and she knew he would not fail. But she would not be a mother if she did not hope against hope her wicked son would renounce his ways, and come home. If they'd turned on the television, they would have picked up the news of the shooting and the death of their boy, Peter. The policeman he had shot lay in hospital, fighting for his life. The surgeon had removed the bullet from his neck, and prayed God would do the rest.

But Amanda and Robert had decided to read quietly and then listen to Rachmaninoff on their sound system - played by Ashkenazy, with the London Symphony Orchestra, conducted by André Previn. And this they did. After wallowing in the stunning performance of The Second Piano Concerto, they decided to go to bed. Robert felt anxious he should not invade Amanda's privacy tonight, considering her trauma earlier in the day, but she made it perfectly clear she needed his love in every way...

'Robert, darling. I want us to make love. We have each other. And I need you...'

And when their love-making was spent, they slept in peaceful, spiritual calm. It was a magical night, a gift from Heaven.

7.55 a.m. and Robert quietly turned on his personal radio in the bathroom. Maybe it was the influence of living on that bloody submarine that had taught him to appreciate small spaces, nooks and crannies and the like - where one could squeeze this and that. Whatever the reason, he now appreciated contact with the outside world more than ever before. Last night had been a one-off, a necessary exercise in incommunicado, of taking stock and caring for Amanda who had stood by him through thick and thin, and who needed him more than she could say. She was still sleeping on in the bedroom, after their special evening together. There was no urgency to rise early, since Sally was now happily ensconced in the running of the boutique, and...

The pips had gone and the newsreader was about to present the 8 o/clock news. Robert turned the volume down even further so as not to awaken Amanda...

'Last night in a London pub frequented by gay men, a young man was shot dead by a police officer, following a distress call from the manager of the establishment. The young man and his gang were all dressed in SS uniforms (here a cold shiver passed through Robert's body, and he feared the worst), and the customers first mistook it for a joke played on them. They soon realized it was no such thing. The young man who appeared to be in charge of the raid aimed a loaded gun at the ceiling of the pub, and silenced the customers into obeying his instructions. When the police arrived, this man, around 19-20 years of age, shot an unarmed officer who fell to the floor. The officer is fighting for his life in the Royal Brompton

Hospital. The rest of the gang, all young men with few previous convictions, have been taken into custody by the police. The dead man is believed to be the younger son of Amanda, the well-known fashion designer.

Now, other news... The government has announced new measures to...'

'God Almighty.' Robert gasped in realization of the facts. It was his own son who had stormed out of this house only last night. Now he was dead, and guilt invaded Robert's being.

But why should he feel guilty? He had been trying to reason with the lad, and he was doing it in a civilized manner with a good whisky apiece. But he did feel guilty. He had mucked it up, botched the inquisition of his son. But why should he blame himself for his inability to make his errant boy co-operate? How was he going to tell Amanda? Understandably, she would be overcome with so much grief, despite Peter's violation of her body, that she'd have every reason to pin the blame on Robert for mishandling his talk with the boy.

But Robert must calm himself. He would let Amanda sleep on until she woke of her own accord. When she knew the facts she'd need all the sleep she could get. And he was still kicking himself for his apparent casual approach to Peter's absence last night... Suddenly, the landline rang downstairs. He tiptoed down to the phone in the drawing-room so as not to disturb Amanda. He picked up the receiver just in time.

'Oh Robert. It's me, Arthur Biggs. Sorry to worry you at this hour, but I wanted to talk to you before I spoke to Amanda. You know the dreadful news, I presume, my friend?'

'Yes, Arthur; heard it on the radio just now,' whispered Robert, ever anxious not to wake Amanda. He explained the situation to Arthur without revealing the incident of rape. He'd only mention this to the authorities with his wife's consent. Her wishes remained paramount.

'My sincere sympathy, Robert.'

'Thank you, Arthur.'

'Now, if there's anything I can do to help, don't hesitate to let me know.'

'Thanks, my friend. I appreciate that.'

'I believe Chief Inspector Lockhart will be dealing with inquiries into this case, Robert. He's a good man; known him for years. He's sensitive, too, so he should give you minimal intrusion. But call me whenever you wish.'

'Thank you again, Arthur. And you, too, are a good man, if you don't mind my saying so. I may give you a call later today. Depends upon Amanda's reaction. As you can imagine, I'm not looking forward to breaking the news to her.'

'My sympathies, Robert. But I know you'll handle it. You are the one person she needs to be with at a time like this.'

'Bless you, Arthur. I intend taking her on a month's holiday as soon as this is over. But she will need to mourn in her own way.'

'I understand. 'Bye for now, my friend.'

''Bye, Arthur.'

Robert tiptoed back up the stairs to the bedroom. To his amazement, Amanda was still fast asleep, breathing contentedly in the warm bed. She looked as beautiful as ever. He would break the news to her as gently as possible, making full use of his own beautiful voice. He should have been an actor, but maybe Adam would beat him to the post. Not that the young man was pursuing the idea. He seemed more keen to become a famous writer. With three published books under his belt he looked forward to the 'Biggy'. And this could be it - the close-to-home novel centred on his mother. It would be a blockbuster, for Robert remained convinced Amanda would tell Adam everything he wanted to know to complete that book. In return, she'd use it as a convenient release, a cleansing of the soul, just as he, Robert, would view the funeral of his son Peter as a necessary cathartic operation, an irreversible disassociation from any form of Nazism.

He sat in a chair by the bed and picked up Amanda's copy of Laurie Lee's 'As I walked out one midsummer morning'. He began to read. He'd never read any of this author's books before now, and he soon found himself irresistibly drawn into the story. Laurie Lee had a gift - a flowing style of narrative, born of a vivid imagination and early talent for poetry. The book gave Robert encouragement: when Amanda recovered sufficient strength after Peter's death and funeral, he would take her on a restful holiday, to the north side of Mallorca - to the Hotel Formentor, to be pampered with superb food and wine, peace and tranquillity. She'd never been there, as far as he knew. But he had. The hotel's reputation remained in the top league: it was famed for catering for famous personages who wanted their privacy respected. Moreover, the spirituality of the surroundings, high up in those magical mountains dropping down to the sea, could hardly fail to touch the sensitive soul. It would be a perfect holiday for them both.

As he mused on that pleasant thought, with full intention of refocusing his eyes on the book, he heard a gentle rustle of the sheets. He looked up, and there was Amanda smiling at him.

'Good morning, my darling.'

'Good morning, my love. Sleep well?'

'Wonderfully, thanks to you. Overdone it a bit, perhaps?'

'You needed the sleep, Amanda. I hope I didn't disturb you?'

'Didn't hear a thing. What's new, then?' She wiped the sleep from her eyes and sat up, her lovely face restored. How could he possibly spoil it with a cruel tale? He took his time, and waited for a signal from her. She studied his face and softly volunteered:

'He's dead, isn't he?'

'How do you know?'

'I can see it in your eyes, darling. You mustn't blame yourself. Just look after me.'

He knew he'd do just that. But how did she know? Was she psychic? Had she dreamt it?

Chapter 34

He could not have hoped for more. The painful job of breaking the devastating news to the one he loved had been borne by another force, an interaction of sensitivity between them, a love and respect which transcended all. The tears would come, without a doubt, at odd intervals and without warning. For his part, Robert would never view emotional outbursts as weakness, even in men. The hardest men in history could cry like a baby when the mood took them. In any case, Amanda and Robert supported each other. They were lucky.

By 11.a.m., they had dealt with a deluge of phone calls - from family, friends, business colleagues and the inevitable 'Nosy Parkers'.

Both Adam and Sally expressed their love and support and offered any practical assistance their parents required of them. Amanda and Robert outlined a probable plan for the funeral, and then, after a quiet holiday, a family get-together in the Oxfordshire manor where they could all let their hair down without restraint.

A call came through from Chief Detective Lockhart as anticipated by Arthur Biggs. He sounded most sympathetic and kind. He said he would call on the Smythe house at 12.30 if that was convenient. It was.

Around 11.am they had brunch of bacon and eggs, sausages and tomatoes, and copious cups of tea And then they discussed the holiday idea that Robert had envisaged while he'd waited for Amanda to awaken from her much needed slumber.

'I think it's a lovely idea, Robert. Let's do it.'

'Fine. I'll book it as soon as we have a date for the funeral.' Oh God, what had he gone and said? Amanda's eyelids flickered as he prepared himself for the first flood of tears. But she recovered herself and requested he keep going. A strong, positive lady indeed. 'Okay, darling, we'll get the detective's visit over with, then I'll get on to the funeral people. Might as well use the same firm you dealt with for another funeral, what was his name? Oh yes, Carl Himmler, wasn't it? Do we know him?' Robert could be quite English at times, and the throw-away remark made her laugh.

At 12.30 sharp, the front door bell rang, and on the step stood Bill Lockhart himself. He sported a smiling, kindly face, superbly wrinkled and creased in the right places as though his job fitted him like a glove. Robert showed him into the drawing-room where Amanda waited to greet him.

With formalities smoothly completed, Inspector Lockhart got down to the nitty-gritty of last night's incident. The inspector kept his report as short as possible, merely referring to the fact young Peter had opened fire first, once at the pub's ceiling, and secondly straight at an unarmed police officer who had given the boy ample time to drop the gun. It was hoped the officer would survive his ordeal and fight for life.

Inspector Lockhart's peroration served its purpose of keeping both Robert's and Amanda's emotions under tight control. It was quite obvious young Peter had pushed his luck too far, and moreover, had not cared what damage or distress to others he would cause in perpetrating his agenda. That said, the inspector showed his human side quite plainly...

'My heartfelt sympathies to you both. I had a son who topped himself with a rope when he was only fifteen. I can really appreciate how you must feel. Unfortunately, we can't win 'em all, as the saying goes. It's a tough world, is it not?'

Amanda and Robert offered their own condolences to Inspector Lockhart whose eyes visibly clouded in thought before reverting to the present. 'Ah well,' he continued, 'life goes on.'

'It does indeed, inspector,' agreed Robert.

'Thank God we have two other superb children,' added Amanda. A credit to Robert and me. They've grown now, of course, with families of their own.'

'That's good,' commented the officer. 'Well, Mr and Mrs Smythe, I did intend asking you whether you had any idea why your younger son should want to do what he did, but I understand if at the moment it might be too upsetting for you to explain.'

'It is rather painful for us, to be honest,' said Robert, shielding his wife, 'but I think we can just tell you we tried our best to steer him from his morbid pursuit of the teachings and philosophy of Hitler's Third Reich. Amanda had caught him avidly reading a 'Nazi' magazine and we both apprehended him about this. I fear he didn't take too kindly to our probing, to say the least. He was a very lonely, insular youngster - quite a different character to the other two when they were his age.'

Amanda knew Robert would not divulge the incident of rape, and they remained grateful for the apparent fact the hospital had kept the press uninformed. There was always the chance of a leak at some stage, but why complicate the situation unnecessarily?

They bid good day to Officer Lockhart, and thanked him for his sensitive, intelligent approach to a stressful event. And they hoped the police officer would win his brave battle for life.

'Thank you, Mr and Mrs Smythe for your kindness. I shall call you if we need to know anything vital in order to wrap up this sad case. My sympathies again. 'Bye for now.'

They saw him depart in his police car, and swish off round the square.

246

Back inside the house, they discussed their next jobs. First, they must organize the funeral. On second thoughts, they agreed it might not be a good idea to use the same funeral director who handled Carl Himmler's last journey. This little job had smacked of the mafia, British style, a 'fixed' affair by the secret services. No, they must employ a regular firm who had no connection with the Himmler case. They found one in the book, and phoned... Yes, they'd heard about the tragedy, but would be pleased to oblige and do the whole thing for Amanda at a reasonable cost. Amanda and Robert agreed, and a date and time was booked for Wednesday of the following week: Golders Green Crematorium was picked.

'Right, darling. That's done. I'll just phone Adam and Sally to inform them, and then we can book our holiday. Any objections?'

'None whatsoever. You go ahead, my love. I know I should be grieving like hell right now, but... well, it may sound an awful thing to say, but Robert, I feel free. I hope and pray to God Peter gets a chance to redeem his soul. But we must go on, you and I together - both in this world and the next. Am I making much sense?'

'Perfect sense to me, Amanda. We've had incredible luck, and we've suffered misfortune, too, yet come through it all - together. It's a great team, you and I. Let's look after and nurture it. Agreed?'

'Agreed, my darling man. Now: Adam's book.'

'What about it?'

'I want to help him write it by giving him all the information he needs. For instance, I feel he should know about the rape, don't you?'

'If you think that's a vital element in his book, darling. It's up to you whether you divulge these intimate yet, I imagine, painful details of your life. I assume you'll try to keep this from Sally?'

'Yes, of course. I don't think she should be saddled with such a revelation. I'm not sure she can handle horror as I imagine Adam can. I may be wrong. If she knew the truth, she might, bless her, allow a slip of the tongue in later life. My feeling is that Adam is able to carry secrets to the grave.'

'I have to agree with you, there, Amanda. Well, if you are happy about sharing this secret, I still think it should be on the basis of a strict undertaking from Adam that, apart from his work of fiction, it goes no further.'

'Agreed, darling.'

'I can sense you're keen for him to write an intensely personal, meaningful book, rather than the average romantic throwaway?'

'Exactly. Let me contact him now, and sound him out on how far he's got with it.'

'Okay, darling, go ahead. Shall I leave you?'

'No, of course not, Robert. We're in this together - unless my intimate details embarrass you?' She glanced at him naughtily, and he laughed. What a woman, he thought.

'Hello, mum. Are you coping with it all? Robert must be a tower of strength to you.'

'He is, my darling boy. We are managing this together. Now, your book... I want to talk to you, intimately.'

'Gosh, mum. D'you think that's wise, over the phone?'

She laughed and went on: 'No, Adam. When I see you next. How far have you got with the book?''

'Well, I've written stuff about the early days when Sally and I were kids, about dad's mock funeral, his confinement on the submarine, his release and the party in the manor with Arthur Biggs and agent Ross.'

'My word, sounds as though you've done heaps of work on it.'

'Yes, mum. In fact, I've written the story up to Peter's rude departure from our family reunion at Brompton Square, remember? He left to go and see a friend, he said, at The Victoria Pub, near Hyde Park Square... But I sense you want to tell me something I need to know, apart from Peter's tragic last night. Am I right?'

'Spot on, Adam. You're a bright lad. Okay. How about Robert and I coming up to the manor this weekend, and we can have a long, long conversation?'

'Great, mum. Shall we expect you Friday night?'

'Hang on, darling. (Aside) Robert, Friday evening at the manor for the weekend?'

'Fine, Amanda. How's around 6, early evening?' (to Adam) 'Around 6 on Friday, Adam?'

'Perfect. I'll put the heating on in the main house and make sure it's clean and comfortable for you. Jill and I will cook a tasty dinner for us all.'

'You're a sweetie, Adam. Love to Jill and young Tom.'

Chapter 35

The weekend at the manor proved to be a great success. Much to Amanda's surprise, Jill's cooking was indeed rather good, helped in part by Adam's delicious sauces, the secret of which he'd picked up from Luigi in the kitchen of 44, Brompton Square, many years before.

After dinner, Jill prepared to put son Tom to bed in her wing of the house. She said she was happy to stay with him until Adam had had a good chat with his parents in the main house, before coming up to bed with her. They could all have another family get-together at breakfast time.

Adam could not have been happier with this arrangement. It meant he could speak to his parents with complete freedom, and he hoped his mother would divulge the information he felt his book needed to give it the final beef. He was getting very excited about it.

In the main drawing-room, over fresh coffees and cognacs (Dalwhinnie whisky for Dad), Amanda began to unwind, and gradually fill in the missing pieces of her saga that would give her son the opportunity of his life. In effect, she was the story-teller, but Adam her son was the writer who would turn it into a tale of love and intrigue for all to read and enjoy.

It was after her third cognac (Robert had begun to worry) that Amanda began to raise her voice as she related her story. On it went - the good, the bad (Adam scribbled furiously on his note-pad) and... there was no indifferent. Life was never like that for Amanda. It was all or nothing. She loathed mediocrity and safety for safety's sake. Her mind was constantly on the move. And now she was on a roll, relating her story for Adam to turn into a blockbuster.

She needed this. She needed to let it all out, to tear open her heart, to these two men in her life. Only her father, David Davidson, the other side of The Pond, could interest her as much as Robert and Adam. Robert had returned to her for good, and they'd picked up the pieces together. Adam had grown and matured but was still her baby boy, her first-born who had dramatically 'become a man' during her marriage to Robert, and who had acted his role with professionalism at Carl Himmler's 'funeral', and had willingly taken on the name of Smythe to identify with his 'risen' father, Robert. Soon he would complete his novel, the one he wanted to write and turn into a bestseller. And Amanda was here to help him... He was listening intently as she at last approached the heated argument she'd had with Peter in London, the argument that preceded Amanda's discovery of her young son's fetish, and then... (Amanda swallowed a large measure of her cognac) her son's hideous rape of her, his own mother - in the full glory of his tight, stunning SS uniform.

She had left nothing out. She had done it for a purpose. It had released her pent up feelings, her anger, her disappointment in Peter, her guilt that he was gone. Adam sat back, knocked for six, but grateful to his brave mother. He knew she had told him the facts to help him write a powerful book, not a harmless, dribbly middle-class woman's story for empty heads. His mother was indeed a woman, but what a woman. His father – more than a very lucky man.

Robert leant over to hold Amanda's hand and squeeze it, and Adam picked up the love between them. It was wonderful to watch. If his own marriage was anything approaching that of his parents he'd count himself a privileged man indeed.

Then she said: 'I wish we'd recorded that. I doubt I could re-enact it, not that I'd want to. Nevertheless, I still wish we'd recorded it.'

Adam smiled. 'We have,' he calmly stated. 'There's a tiny mike in the arm of that chair, mum. Hope you forgive the deception.'

'I do indeed, Adam. But you'd better keep it under lock and key. Only you and Robert should know the reality of those reckless words and emotions of mine. But then, that's how it was.'

'Mama dear, you're one in a million. I have my book. I just have to put it all together. And 1 don't want you to worry. It's gonna be good. I've changed the names as I said I would, and when you two come back from your well-deserved holiday, we'll have a party here, shall we?'

'Yes, darling.'

'I'll ring my agent Monday morning. He's expecting a gutsy book from me. This is it, I'm sure.' Adam walked over to kiss his mother and father and offer them a 'final' night-cap.

'Well, darling, I should say no, but your interview has taken a bit out of me.' Amanda felt as though a huge weight had been miraculously removed from her soul for ever.

The funeral, thank God, was soon over and done with. A few tears of grief and shame were shed by the Smythe's, and then it was time to move on.

The papers had their say and then looked for another horror on which to gloat and entertain a morbid public.

Then at last came their vacation in Mallorca at the Hotel Formentor, high up on the north side of the island. They had hired a car from Hertz, and picked it up at Palma Airport. It was fabulous weather, and they drove up across the island, stopping at little cafès and bars as the mood took them. There was no hurry. This would be a holiday they'd never forget, and when it was over,

Adam would show people the photos of his parents, looking bronzed, happy, and still in love.

The vacation passed all too quickly, but then, in less than another month it was time for the big 'do' at the manor. It would be a party where they could all let go.

Amanda and Robert were delighted David Davidson could join them. Amanda had told her father nothing of the story relating to Peter's outrage upon her. She could not be sure he could take the truth. It was enough his support for the whole family remained as constant as ever, and she was glad he was prepared to make the journey to the UK. Arthur Biggs, too, had accepted the invitation, "for old times' sake." Sadly, agent Ross had recently passed away, not in suspicious circumstances as Adam had imagined but from cirrhosis of the liver. No one had thought he'd drunk that much at the manor when Robert had been released from the sub, and they had celebrated over a dinner with the young Adam firing pertinent questions at him. But it just goes to show: perhaps he had been behaving himself in the presence of the children, as a one-off exercise in self-control before reverting to his normal drinking pattern that would afford him a surprisingly long life.

Robert had invited Commander McGregor who had 'retired' from the service, and it was hoped he would turn up to enjoy the special occasion. After all, Robert had savoured those discussions on the submarine that had preserved his sanity, assisted, without doubt, by the flow of Dalwhinnie whisky. That was certainly a blessed introduction to a gentle spirit.

Sally and Raymond also said they'd be delighted to attend. Amanda assured Sally there'd be plenty of room for them all to stay over night.

The evening was upon them, and with tables laid, the candles flickering their welcoming, romantic light, the liquid voice of Nat King Cole drifting subtly through the ether of the sound-system, and so many happy faces jostling around her, Amanda surveyed the scene with palpable pleasure. She looked simply stunning in her new dress – one of her own designs – a full-length black velvet creation with finely embossed orchid highlights around the hem-line. A diamond necklace, a few simple rings on the fingers, lovely flowing hair, and of course that radiant smile completed the picture. Robert, for his part, remained her perfect consort. He'd lived with the 'Cruise' image for quite a while, it seemed. It would be a shame to lose it completely, despite the fact he was so much taller than the famous actor. He looked great, and still walked with that superb elegance and confidence that had first attracted Amanda all those years ago in Morton's.

As for the children, well, they were no longer youngsters - Adam and Sally with their spouses and little ones, all looking cheerfully excited. A tangible vibrancy filled the room as the candlelight played shadows over the tapestries. Would Sally see one of her ghosts tonight, or had she other matters to occupy her these days?

Speech, speech. Yes, it was true. David Davidson had been called upon to speak. He still had the presence and that fine, rich voice and manner of delivery, perfect for occasions such as these. And he knew it. So why be churlish and refuse to oblige on his own daughter's special night? He'd do it for her.

He stood up in his place, and addressed the gathering, beaming away his pleasure in being home once more in the old country. It was good to see Amanda back with... He'd hold his counsel tonight, in front of all these people. Just in case.

'Ladies and Gentlemen, boys and girls. What a happy picture we have - set in this beautiful Elizabethan manor house, so elegantly furnished and lit for us oldies and young alike. I am so proud to be here - to rejoin my daughter Amanda and Robert in their joy, to be with my grandson Adam and his wife and son Tom, my granddaughter Sally and her husband and children, and of course our honoured guests who have come from far and wide to be here with us this evening.

Now, tonight is a very special occasion, not only as a celebration of the love between Amanda and Robert, but also the publication of a new book by my grandson Adam (murmurs of delight circulated the room as Amanda's face lit up). I am told it's a work of fiction, and I know Adam possesses a vivid imagination. Yet I suspect if one is clever enough to read between the lines, those seeds of truth will surely emerge and be recognized: at least by the initiated.' David faced the applauding gathering with a wicked grin. 'And now I call upon Adam himself to do his own thing.'

Adam rose to even louder applause, and waited patiently for it to subside. He was still smiling at his parents as his mother wiped away those welling tears and looked up to his handsome face. He held a signed copy of the book in his hand, and, looking straight into her eyes as he bent down, he presented it to her with his tender title words: 'To Mama, With Love.'

'Thank you, my darling,' she said as she hugged him close. Then, as she glanced at the book, written in her honour, she spotted the author's name. 'Um,' she commented humorously, 'an innocent enough nom de plume, I think, Adam. Was Anthony Sharp one of your more eccentric friends from Oxford days?'

Epilogue

Amanda and Robert lived on into their nineties, and were buried in an Oxfordshire churchyard where Adam and Sally continued to place flowers and shed genuine tears of loss and gratitude. They hoped and prayed their own long lives reflected at least a little of the warmth and courage of their parents, these two extraordinary human beings who had found real love and strength together 'for better and for worse'.

About The Author

Anthony Sharp was educated at his local grammar school in London, and went up to Oxford as the Organ Scholar of Lincoln College, sharing tutorials with his contemporary and fellow Londoner, Dudley Moore, who had won The Organ Scholarship at Magdalen College.

While Dudley's career blossomed into great achievements, fame and fortune, Anthony's struggled for survival in a whirlpool of disappointment and self-inflicted disasters. There were a few compensations in the form of TV appearances and concert hall recitals on London's South Bank. Yet his unhappy stint as University Organist back at Oxford could hardly compare with the depravities of London night clubs where, from the piano stool, he could survey the antics of 'grown' men and women.

Little wonder, then, that he should one day enjoy writing humorous, highly individual paperbacks, and to hell with it all.

His first novel, 'The Guv'nor', was published by Regency Press in London. There followed 'The House of Baghdad' and 'Lie Back & Think of England', both published by Author House, USA. Then came 'NOW OR NEVER', also published by Author House and a sequel to 'The Guv'nor', involving not only Prince Charles but also President Barack Obama, Lewis Hamilton and Osama Bin Laden, a book perhaps to really set the cat amongst those proverbial pigeons. But then, Anthony Sharp is hardly an author for readers seeking a non-challenging comfort zone.

For details of all these books visit his website –
www. bookswithalaugh. co. uk

Printed in Great Britain
by Amazon